THE KEY TO REALITY

"ILARIE VORONCA" was the pen name of Eduard Marcus (1903-1946), one of the greatest avant-garde writers of his time. A Jewish Romanian by birth, he published numerous texts in his home country before permanently establishing himself in France, where he produced volumes of poetry and prose in the French language, including *L'Apprenti fantôme et Cinq poèmes de septembre* (1938), *La Confession d'une âme fausse* (1942), and *Souvenir de la planète Terre* (1945).

SUE BOSWELL studied French Language and Literature at UCL and for a time taught French at Goldsmiths University of London. She then moved into university administration, specialising in external relations and communications. Later she became a translator for the Wiener Holocaust Library, and translated Arnaud Rykner's novel *Le Wagon* as *The Last Train* (Snuggly Books, 2020). Her other translations include Marcel Schwob's *The Assassins and other Stories*, Ilarie Voronca's *The Confession of a False Soul* and with her husband, Colin Boswell, Gustave Kahn's *The Mad King*, also for Snuggly Books. Sue and Colin live in London and Ouveillan, a village near Narbonne in the Languedoc.

BRENDAN CONNELL has published numerous works of fiction and translations. The former include *Unpleasant Tales* (Eibonvale Press, 2013). His translations include Guido Gozzano's *Alcina and Other Stories* (Snuggly Books, 2019).

SNUG
OKS

ILARIE VORONCA

THE KEY TO REALITY

TRANSLATED BY

SUE BOSWELL

AND WITH AN INTRODUCTION BY

BRENDAN CONNELL

THIS IS A SNUGGLY BOOK

ISBN: 978-1-64525-091-3

CONTENTS

INTRODUCTION

Eduard Marcus, who wrote under the pen name of "Ilarie Voronca," was born into a Jewish family on 31st December 1903, in the eastern Romanian town of Brăila, and died by suicide on 8th April 1946, in Paris.

Voronca's early poems, symbolist in tone, were published in the avant-garde magazine *Sburătorul*, in 1922. Under the influence of a modernist manifesto published in *Contimporanul*, another Romanian avant-garde magazine, however, he quickly changed his style and, in 1924, together with his like-minded friends Victor Brauner and Stephan Roll, published a single-issue review called *75 HP* which, with its striking red and black format, was remarkable for the typographical and graphic audacity it displayed.

Upon receiving his law degree in 1925, Voronca moved to Paris, where he was hired by the Abeille insurance company, and two years later, in 1927, published *Colomba*, a volume of poetry, named after his wife, which was his first clear venture into surrealism. In 1928 another book of poetry, *Ulise*, was released, which contained an illustration by Marc Chagall showing the author as the Eiffel Tower, and then in 1929 *Plante si animale*, with illustrations by Constantin Brancusi. All three of these books were published in Romanian by the Imprimerie Union, a press established in Paris by Volf Chalit and Dimitri Snégaroff, two Russian Jews whose publishing venture was geared towards the Eastern European immigrant community in France.

In 1929 Voronca returned to Romania, where he lived and published for the next four years, before establishing himself permanently in France, in 1933. The following year saw the publication of *Poèmes parmi les hommes*, the first of his books to be written in French, the language in which, from this point forward, all his books were written. In all, during his lifetime, he published seventeen books in French—volumes of poetry, short stories, and novels.

La Clé des réalités, expertly translated in the present volume under the title *The Key to Reality*, was Voronca's only collection of short fiction, being published two years after the novel *La Confession d'une âme fausse* (translated as *The Confession of a False Soul*, Snuggly Books 2021), in January 1944, in the midst of the second world war, by Méridien, a small publishing house specialising in avant-garde works—contemporaneously with another fantastic novel, *L'Interview*, published by the Marseille publisher Jean Vigneau. It is possible that much of the material in the collection had been previously published in various journals, but access to many such items being restricted on-line due to copyright, searching them out would be difficult. The environment in which the book was published, however, should be kept in mind, the volume, before to going to print, having passed through the hands of "Censure No. 8606", who probably was unaware that Voronca was not only Jewish, but also engaged in activities with the French resistance.

—Brendan Connell

THE KEY TO REALITY

THE KEY TO REALITY

For Denys-Paul Bouloc[1]

. . . What I would have liked to know was what we do down on earth to earn a place in the great beyond.

As a child I would enjoy watching from the rustic steps the trains passing with their metallic rattling in front of the house. Those trains were like clock hands marking the passage of the days. The goods trains were always greyish, panting and heavy, looking as if they were climbing an imaginary slope. They would start coming past very early in the morning when the night mists had not yet dispersed and they never managed to throw off the soot of darkness. But the express would pass by at five o'clock in the afternoon always bursting with light and joy. It rushed by at great speed and I would have just enough time to catch sight of its glis-

---

1 Denys-Paul Bouloc (1918-2005), French journalist, author and poet, and editor of Voronca's volumes of poems. Also a member during World War II, with Voronca, of the Resistance in Rodez, Aveyron, and joint founder of the Association des Ecrivains de Rouergue (Writers' Association of Rouergue).

tening panes which in the whirlwind of speed merged into a single window. The express always had lights on inside. And it was the express which showed me the advance of autumn and then winter. Suddenly I would notice that it was coming past in darkness when the previous day it had still been in full sunshine. "Ah! It's November already!" and I would be astonished to hear I was talking to myself. It was dark at five o'clock. But the express would shine amid the seasons, more proudly, more ornate with its lights. Like a shooting star, its impression would remain in my vision for a long time. The air surrounding this rapid passage of happiness was also joyful. The silent house and courtyard around me would sink back into their gloomy melancholy. The walls would shake from top to bottom. They loved to be wrapped in this smoke shawl. As we were on the outskirts of the village my only companions were the shouts of the woodcutters. My mother would appear briefly: "Aren't you cold, little one? Still watching the trains?" There were trains manoeuvring to change tracks. Somewhere the signal box would decide, with a sharp crack, on the direction of a convoy. These wagons remained. But those disappearing in the distance, in the rapid passage of the express, where were they going? The names of the great capitals passed through my head: London, Berlin, Paris. The five o'clock express came from Istanbul, going to London via Calais. You see, I said to myself, those people in there! By whose order? And how can they be certain that they'll arrive at their destination? Even if I can't continue to watch them, they will continue to exist, they move about, they talk, they laugh.

Every day I would take up my observation post. I would watch wide-eyed. I would follow the express as far as I could. Until it disappeared, swallowed up by distance with its cargo of men. You put one foot on the step, you heave yourself up onto the platform and that's it, you're on board. It's the train which takes over, carries you off 'elsewhere'.

Since that time I have been afraid. I knew a single gesture could commit me for ever. When later, as a young man, I would bury my face in fern-flavoured hair, I could still sense the trains lying in wait for me. To lean over a face where two surprised eyes are looking at you, that is to be committed. To dip your lips in a brook's water is to be committed too! Laughing in the sunshine, is to be committed. Stroking a gazelle's delicate head. Arriving one morning at a town's gates when the street sweepers are throwing the remains of the night into the gutter, when the shops are greeting each other with the hoarse and sleepy voice of their iron drapes, when you want to lie down, if only on a carpet of grass to stop the peaceful waters of darkness leaving.

Sometimes I would sit down in the public gardens towards evening, as everything was calming down, when people were lowering the flame of their hatred, when they were hiding their eyes so as not to scare the misty birds of twilight. Once I saw an old man sprawling on a bench, his face melting away in the shadows, his clothes only just held up by his body as it gradually faded away. I was still very young at that time and I could not stop myself saying to the old man: "I admire and respect you for having the strength and tenacity to get to your age."

"How old do you think I am?"

"Seventy."

"I'm ninety," he replied, smiling.

"You really don't look it."

"And yet my life has not always been fun."

"I believe you," I replied, "for I, who am still young, have already been tempted, many times, to put an end to it. How have you managed to hold on, not to let yourself be destroyed?"

"I didn't do much; I lived, I allowed myself to live."

The square was gradually emptying. In the trees, the birds' racket was dying down and silence was like a spider spreading its web to catch some last sounds. I remembered then that everywhere at this time trains were passing each other. Long lines of lorries followed each other along the roads. Express trains, buses criss-crossed the earth's crust. Elsewhere, animals migrated from one place to another. Flocks of birds moved around the skies. Rivers full of fish rushed towards the estuaries. Barges laden with coal, grain, fruit journeyed towards the sea. Yes, we were sitting there on a bench and during this time the whole world was on the move. Neither evening, nor autumn, nor regret, nor melancholy could slow that fever of the world. All thirst after something, all are running, all are anxious to arrive. But to arrive where? Which path are they following? The old man and I were sitting there watching the evening light shredding itself amid the branches and elsewhere men were rushing wildly about hither and thither.

Just now, in the square, there were still peaceful women and children. But the children will grow up and will refuse to come here to dream. They too will crowd into trains, into boats, they will skim over the waves, the distant clouds.

Surely at this very moment there is still a child, at the place where I used to stand years before, watching the dizzying passage of an express. Perhaps that child is still myself, for, contrary to accepted belief, we do not grow up, we multiply, we become an infinity of different beings who if they were to meet would no longer recognise each other. At every moment we become someone else and the being we were before is left behind, and forgets us. One day someone will come and take us by the hand and lead us along with pathways of the world, showing us such and such beings and saying: "That one is you. And that one there is also you. That child staring at the grey landscape where trains pass is you. And that tall adolescent who is teased by his friends for his awkwardness because he has grown too quickly, who is sitting hunched on a school bench, that's also you. That labourer at a building site, with his ragged clothes and his sweat mingling with the mortar, that's you again. That employee who is only separated by a window from the cheerful street but from which he is estranged by centuries of subjugation, that's you again; and that man at the height of his powers who speaks bitter words to a noble and good woman whose heart he is breaking, that's you too. And that other man kneeling before a prostitute who beats him with her impure hands, that's also you." "They are me, all those? And he whose hand you are holding and who you are speaking to at this moment, who is he then?" "You again." And you walk away in the same way as all those who you were previously.

Yes, I see myself in the guise of these countless beings, I see "us" for "I" am a thousand others. Thus every gesture becomes definitive. Every being who is or has been me is eternal. So, every step, every look commits me. And the child, the adolescent, the young man, the old man remain for ever as they appear to be: unchanging. For movement does not exist. No, there is no movement: it is a succession of superimposed images. They are the hundreds, the thousands of the beings we are, following each other like a film strip and giving the illusion of movement. We are forever in the same place, that is to say everywhere. Outside time. For time does not exist. We are space. We are the heavens.

But where are they then, all these "me" that I have lost? Who makes them suffer, and who do they make suffer? Simultaneously executioners and victims, our hearts are ripped out by violent hands whilst our own hands are plunged into the breast of another.

Oh! Noble old man, perhaps all we are doing is chasing our own shape and which only those can achieve who overcome the dangers and attain an age like yours. I would like to question you but I keep quiet so as not to frighten you with my questions. In short, what I would like to ask you as you near the end of your journey is to tell me what has been of wonder to you, what is the unforgettable thing that you have glimpsed and which gave you the will to live. Here I am on the bench next to you, clumsy, looking for words, without managing to make myself understood. You are serene. No noisy stork comes to disturb the water of your meandering gaze. I still have years to live. I could even start all over again. But how to go about it? Certainly, amongst the thousands of beings that we are over the course of our existence and which are born and die at the same time, there must be one who is the chosen one, who is really who we are and of which the other beings are nothing but a pale reflection. Which one is it? If one of us knew he could say: "I am complete!" and like an oak tree with its glorious halo of birds he could sink into the earth and await the loving thunderbolt of his destiny.

But, handsome old man, you were perhaps the head of a business, brutal and energetic, ordering your employees about in a rough voice. If so, I revile and curse you.

You were perhaps a usurer, exchanging the wedding ring of an abandoned wife for a dish of lentils. If so, I revile and curse you.

You were perhaps the captain who instead of taking care of the men in his charge deprives them of their pittance and grows rich on their hunger. If so, I revile and curse you.

You were perhaps the building owner who closes the door to the homeless. If so, I revile and curse you.

You were perhaps the chairman or director, listening rapturously in a luxurious office to a report on production, but not on the noise, heat and dust of the machines. If so, I revile and curse you.

Ah! I opened their doors a little and saw them comfortably installed in their soft armchairs, wearing silk and gold, presiding like priests, with eyes like crickets burning in their oily faces. Ah! Too far away, too distant, for the men busily working to notice and recognise them. Surrounded by the high walls of their laws and their privilege. Laughing among themselves, sharing the lands, the harvest, the fish-filled waters, the mountains with their free and joyful echoes. I have seen them losing their temper and storming against some subordinate trying to go against their orders. No pity for the man with calloused soot- and clay-blackened hands. No pity for the humble man, condemned to toil and poverty.

One day an unknown man approaches. Amazed, he looks at the trees, the houses, the hills. He stops, surprised, at the doors to narrow courtyards where men and women are busy. Behind counters, in the shops, men are bent over ledgers, adding up figures. In huge buildings in the town centre a noisy crowd is milling around. Men run up staircases, with papers under their arms. Names and more figures are being marked up on blackboards. Administrators gather in big boardrooms. Directors talk on the telephone, their voices hoarse, dictating their orders. And the stranger is astonished by it all. "So am I like you? What on earth is making you so excited? Your dossiers in which your lives are yellowing more than autumn leaves do not interest me. I thought to start with that you were taking part in a game. But no, you're not playing. You take yourselves seriously. Your calculations are of no interest to me. Nor the progress of your business. Nor the letters which you write to your inspectors and to your agents. Nor your buying and selling methods." And the stranger wipes his face with his hand as if to obliterate the dirty stain of this vision. Dreamily, he goes along a garden path. He picks a few redcurrants which shine in his open palms like morning drops of blood. Ah! Tell him the names of your trees—you have forgotten the perfumes of your clouds, tell him the colours of your seasons. How will you manage to keep him amongst you, you whose voices have forgotten the words of heaven and of stone and can no longer utter anything but the sterile sounds of your wealth. Oh! Wretched living beings, have you not seen how the dead despise you? Have you not seen how they turn away and dissociate themselves from you, how they are strangers to you, how nothing coming from you can any longer touch them? Ah! Laugh or cry, tear off your clothes, scratch your faces, the dead are no longer watching you. Your debates, your petty disputes, the things you share, your adventures, your factories, your ships, your relationships, are no longer of any interest to them. Suddenly they're getting away from you, they're turning their faces towards a splendour so great that nothing which constitutes your lives has any attraction for them anymore. A stranger comes one day amongst you. A dead person rises one day and comes amongst you. He is amazed. He calls to the rivers. And he calls to you: "Look!": but you don't hear him.

I shall make a great bonfire of your archives
I shall turn your offices, your factories, into ruins,
I shall tear down your sheds, your barns, your depots,
Where you build walls, I shall bring clouds

Ah! I know your lies, your ploys. I do not want
Your money or your fame
I shall pulverise your machines
My brother the wind, my sister the flood will come to my
[aid.

Damn you all! To nothingness all your works! I despise
Your due dates, your unpaid banker's drafts, your backdated
Receipts. I have no interest in your insurance
Policies, your deeds of ownership, your mortgages

With whips of fire I shall oust you
From the universe's high-pillared temple
I shall smash open your safes, I shall wash
The stones soiled by your greedy gaze.

Come to my side, divine anger, O Tempests!
And if these wicked beings appear humble
If they become pale, if they lower their eyes, if they seem
Repentant, do not be moved to pity

For straightaway afterwards they will recover their pride
They will construct again their walls of self-regard
They will put their brothers in chains
They will crucify those who speak to them of God and of love.

Space, there will be space here
Vast gardens, offerings, galas
Together we shall build other cities
Where no worm shall lodge beneath liberty's stone.

⁂

I had not spoken. I had just thought all that. But the old man looked as if in his silence he had heard everything. There were several of us now, for our unspoken conversation had attracted a few of the square's lingering dreamers. An old woman, her head wrapped in a scarf, spoke up, saying:

I'm a char woman and I clean offices once they're closed. I arrive around 6.30 in the evening, for the employees, although they are supposed to leave at 6 o'clock, sometimes hang around to please their boss. Some even stay at their desks for a long time afterwards, so that I never manage to do the cleaning properly. It's as if they're jealous and they resent anyone touching their files. There are stacks of them, covered in dust, in cupboards, on bookcases, on shelves, on chairs and tables and even on the floor. The waste-paper baskets too are full. The drawers are overflowing with letters. What can there be in them that's so precious? I looked at a few of them. They were all the same. They said they had the honour of confirming receipt of such and such a sum or of remitting such and such a sum. The words written there looked awkward, embarrassed. The figures, Oh! The figures reigned supreme in all their glory. Words no longer had any meaning. They were ashamed to be words, they would have preferred to be more like figures. Besides, they had practically become figures. They did not conjure up the sky, nor the wind, nor the gardens, nor strolls with a loved one. It was a question solely of paying in cheques, signatures, legacy documents, guarantees, overdue interest, summonses, expert reports, book-keeping, honoraria.

One evening I went into the Director's office without knocking. He had not yet left, and not expecting to be caught unawares he was putting small packets away in a secret cupboard. There were bundles of bank notes alongside boxes of sweets and dried fruits, bottles of perfume, cigarettes with gold tips, medals, pens.

"You see," he couldn't help confessing to me, once he had got over his surprise at my intrusion, "these are the marks of affection shown by my staff and my agents. I tell them from time to time to think of me, and they send or bring me little titbits or nice things." As I was wanting to leave he led me to another corner of the room. (What urge to confess had taken hold of him?) There was there a small piece of kit rather like a telephone. He pressed a button and some small cages appeared looking like a beehive. In them you could see many small figures, some having dinner, others at a bar counter, others sitting in a cinema seat, others bent over a table covered in files. "You see," the Director said to me, "I'm taking you into my confidence showing you all this. Only the top directors of important companies have this piece of equipment. It shows how the employees pass their time once they leave the office: and it tells me which are those who care about my business and which work for the success of my company whilst at home too. One day I shall promote those to junior directorships and perhaps, amongst them, there may be one who will become a senior director."

Then he showed me a small hidden window through which a special arrangement of lenses allowed you to see all the work rooms: this one is the typing pool. And you could see a huge hall with sixty or so small chairs and tables in several rows. The room was empty and the typewriters with their black covers looked like small coffins. "Ah," the Director said to me, "can you understand how happy it makes me when during working hours I see the young women busy typing up their shorthand notes. By a special piece of kit I can even hear the tapping of their keys." And suddenly, realising he'd said too much, he sent me away. "Go on," he said to me, "and get on with your work."

The next day the cashier told me I'd been replaced. And since that day, no other company has wanted to take me on. From time to time I find it hard working for private individuals and I only earn just enough to keep me from starving to death.

My story is a sadder one, said a young ill-shaven man with threadbare clothes and a stoop. Listen to this: after long months working in a bank I got a week's leave which I decided to spend in the Alps. I wrote to a family boarding house which I had often visited when I was younger and better off. It was a place famous for its spa waters and the beauty of its setting beside Lake Geneva. From my small room in the villa overlooking the lake I could see the lights of Switzerland at the other side of the water. On the evening of my arrival, when I had unpacked my cases, I lingered a while on the terrace and then went to sit at the table which had been reserved for me in the smart dining room.

Around me there were couples talking in low voices, their gestures spreading a scent of calm happiness in the air. Three sides of the room had large French windows opening on to a garden where the lake and the moon glowed among the fir trees like a hint of snow to come. It was the end of August and although the days were still long, they were breathing their last and twilight was falling to bring a refreshing weariness. In the room with its blinding white tablecloths, its crystal and its sparkling cutlery, waitresses moved around gracefully, anticipating the slightest wish of the visitors. How far all that was from the musty restaurants where for the past year I had been taking my rushed meals. There, lunch hours were like a punishment. You needed hunger's sharp stimulus to persuade you to eat at a small table, hemmed in by desperate and ugly fellow diners who got the glasses or forks mixed up or often confused your napkin for theirs. We were all there, like starving dogs, whilst the proprietor, grown fat on the misery of his clients, passed amongst us, his voice like the sharp crack of a whip and waving his beringed hands about. But here, all was restful and the friendly hotelier would come to ask each person if the meal was to their taste. On my right and my left smiling young women dined with their companions.

I was embarrassed at being alone, for solitude is also an indication of poverty. All over the room there were tables with several people around them: Here, a fiancé full of consideration for his fiancée. Further away, a young married man with his affectionate wife. Or young parents with their children glowing with happiness. I was captivated by this safe and carefree atmosphere. Invisible ties were already forming between me and these charming neighbours. To my left, at the far end of the room near the French window, at a table laden with good things and with his back towards me, sat a solitary gentleman. I noticed him with some fellow feeling for, like me, he had no one to share his meal with. I could see his bald head and the wrinkles at the back of his neck and guessed he was middle-aged. A bottle of vintage wine in a basket covered with the dust of many years completed the still life of brightly coloured plates and glasses. He was sitting stiffly, and his gestures seemed studied in advance. He seemed to be attacking his dinner as methodically as he did everything he undertook. I was struck by the fact that there were two places laid at his table and that before serving himself he would hold the dish out courteously, as if someone was sitting in front of him. The sympathy which I had felt for this person to start with out of a sense of solidarity in our loneliness gradually evaporated. I turned my gaze towards the other guests and exchanged smiles with them. By the time dinner was over this silent conversation between contented people had already made me some friends. On the terrace, watching the splendid sunset, I joined in with some groups and exchanged cordial words with my new friends. Hey presto! I could feel myself being reborn. And even if as I leaned over the balustrade I waved to my reflection in the water of the lake, I no longer recognised myself. I had forgotten that I was capable of being a joyful and smiling young man, talking to kindly friends about sweet nothings. Was that really me, saying things that the young women reacted to with laughter and who, as the sun slid behind the distant hills, was feeling free and happy? No misery now tugged at my soul. I was no longer the fearful employee sadly carrying out his work and failing to escape from the pincer-like clutches of his lifetime's regrets.

"Sunsets and sunrises are not the same," I heard myself saying, and a new confidence took hold of me as I saw that I was listened to with goodwill. "No, nature's spectacles are not the same in sadness as in joy. Here, amongst these people and their affectionate hospitality—it's true, at the cost of our lodging, but this cost is reasonable—the sun as it sets puts on its most precious lacework, casts its scarlet lilies, lights up the carnations, it shakes the mountain tops and a golden dust scatters through the air. The greyish twilight, and the ragged sun dimly lighting the sad streets of work, are far away. Why would nature show her glorious finery to the poor man, the despairing man who has nothing but a piece of dry bread? Those blessed by providence, and my friends, we are amongst them at this moment, let us rejoice that we are entitled to the finest fruits, that we have a sacred right to the landscapes, to the wonderful sites illuminated by the stars of day and of night. Tumbledown walls, a consumptive sky, leprous trees amongst the gratings of a deserted boulevard—that would be fine for the little people of this world. But for the bigger ones: magnificent vistas, alpine gorges, rivers of foam and starlight, bright colours escaping from the open hands of dawn. Do not the fortunate people of this world come across the dawn, as after a night spent partying and drinking they leave the mansion of one of their friends to go back to their own? Then the dawn gives off a happy feeling, it charms them with its sparkling dew, with the flowers of its splendid sky. But think of the labourer or the low-level employee, drowsy because he hasn't slept well in his cluttered and stuffy little room, making his way to the kitchen: dawn quickly hides its precious tissues, it becomes then the dustman or shabby rag and bone man rummaging in the bins. Ah! How ugly the world is! exclaims the poor man and his heart bleeds as he looks at the windows the colour of cinders, his feet sliding on the hostile pavement, as the rising sun already weighs him down, facing the day's dreary work. And the beautiful seascape! Have you thought of that? Imagine the docker, the porter, the coalminer bowed down beneath too heavy sacks. For them, the sea has a beggar's filth and repulsiveness. For them, the sky is cloudy, for them the trees become stunted and the salty air, so vivifying for the others, is bitter and harmful for their lips, already parched by fatigue. At the same time, for the leisured classes, for the stroller, for the carefree stockholder, the landscape rapidly takes on its most precious qualities. Go on, go on, my friends—for the poor person anything is good. Look in old drawers for outdated coupons, it's not worth getting out the jewels, the velvet, the silks. Let us be proud, we people, as we face this twilight which in our honour is so generous and spectacular. It doesn't matter to us if, a few steps from here, in his tumble-down hut, a fisherman's exhausted apprentice, ill-treated by his master, views his evening filled with sadness and tatters."

And this was how I let myself be carried away by an easy lyricism. I was discovering that I could be passionate. Were they not listening to me, these holiday companions? A young woman was looking at me dreamily, her tiny hand clutching her husband's arm. Thus I had forgotten my own miserable condition; I was breathing deeply, I had my eyes open to the world.

Standing apart from the groups, distant and taciturn, was the character whose solitude I had noticed at dinner. The lamps were lit in the garden and I could now see his face. Clean-shaven, bespectacled, wearing a sporty outfit with plus fours, he looked like a teacher or a minor scientist used to laboratory calculations. Looking at him, so sure of himself, with his steely gaze, gave me no pleasure. This man almost scared me. I turned away.

I met him the next day, and the day after that, always as cold and distant. It was obvious that this man was avoiding making acquaintance. Wearing shorts this time; his legs were covered in white hairs, his rump prominent, and he paddled around in a canoe somewhere, not reappearing until mealtimes. He would peruse the wine list methodically, selecting the most prestigious to order.

Cautiously and not revealing my own feelings, I mentioned him to a young couple whose room was next to his.

"He's an uncouth character," they said to me. "He has a way of disturbing our sleep, banging the door, leaving the tap running, talking loudly. He must be a junior manager in some company or other treating himself to a fancy holiday. Even his name is off-putting. It's Impavidus. Sometimes during the night we hear a woman's voice in his room. We've never seen him with anybody. So he must be hiding some pathetic affair with someone so ugly he's embarrassed to be seen with her."

My friends were getting carried away, giving free rein to their indignation and even though I shared their opinion I was nevertheless surprised at such ferocity.

At lunchtime on the day after this conversation I was sitting at my table. Mr. Impavidus came trotting through the middle of the room without any greeting, to his place near the French window.

He perused the wine list for a long time and ordered his meal with affected and unnatural head movements. I was about to turn away to look elsewhere when, to my astonishment I noticed in a beam of sunshine coming through the open window a young woman of great beauty sitting opposite Mr. Impavidus. I hadn't seen her arrive. But was I dreaming? For here was the man leaning towards the woman's ear—and she moving away quickly in fright, her chair moving out of the sunbeam and I could no longer see her. Mr. Impavidus was alone once more. So had I been the victim of an illusion and had the beautiful face I had glimpsed been nothing but a memory stirred up from somewhere as the wind stirs up pollen? I could no longer tear my eyes away from the table, I kept watch like a sentinel, not eating properly, replying vaguely to those who spoke to me. I was in danger of losing the goodwill I had just aroused, but that had little importance. I wanted to know. After a few minutes the woman had moved without thinking and was back in a beam of light which made her visible. This time I saw only a part of her face—the rest having remained in the invisibility zone—and some black curls. A very white arm reached for the water carafe and I could feel on my lips the freshness of both. Thus, on several occasions I saw now the forehead, now the shoulder, now the hair or the eyes of Mr. Impavidus's beautiful companion. I had already formed a precise idea and begun to shake with rapture when Mr. Impavidus got up from the table, crossed the room alone and disappeared into the garden.

"Did you see the beautiful woman sitting at the table of your room neighbour?"

"Your sense of irony is doubly wicked," replied the young married couple to whom I spoke these words, "for Mr. Impavidus lunched alone as usual." I refrained from telling them what I had seen and set off in search of my hero. He was walking through the trees. Then, as on the other afternoons, he fetched his canoe and at the spot where the villa threw a fairly thick shade—the lake being to the north-west—he got into it. For a while he followed the shady bank and I soon lost sight of him. For the rest of the day I imagined the most unlikely happenings.

What could he be hiding then, this character I had taken for a teacher? And who was this woman whose voice the neighbours had heard and whose face I had seen in a moment's bright light? I waited impatiently for evening. But at dinner time I saw that the strange individual, as if he had been warned, had changed tables. He was no longer visible to me. I tried in vain to discover some new clue. With his usual studied gestures Mr. Impavidus ordered a bottle of pricey wine, and, in his haughty way and without ever looking around him, he ate his meal. His table was in a circle of shade and I could not tell if anyone else was sitting there.

Before going to bed I passed his door several times. Was I going to knock? As a pretext for an unexpected visit I had decided to name the neighbours who had offered me their friendship! Finally, I took my courage in both hands, and with a beating heart I scratched rather than knocked at the door and, without waiting for a response from inside, partially opened it. On the threshold I stopped, struck dumb with astonishment. In the middle of the room, turning towards me, her hair loose, was a woman of incomparable beauty. Her eyes expressed joy and fear at the same time. She moved towards me, had just enough time to whisper "Tomorrow morning at seven o'clock," and went quickly towards the toilet, from which the man who intrigued me now made an appearance, his expression grim. "What do you want?" he asked me roughly, as the woman in whose direction he threw a withering look vanished behind him and into the small room. I mumbled my excuses, naming the neighbours, and left.

You can imagine the impatient night I passed. I would look at my watch every half hour. At last dawn broke, I was tired out. I got dressed and at seven o'clock I knocked at Mr. Impavidus's door. Someone responded by knocking from the inside. Then I heard a sort of whisper. "Bend down," the voice was saying to me. "Put your ear to the keyhole." The hotel staff were starting to move around. Shoes were still outside doors. I was risking being caught. But I did not hesitate. The door was locked. "Open up," I said quietly.

"I can't. I don't have the key."

I did as the woman asked: I put my ear to the keyhole. Now I could clearly hear her frightened voice; she spoke quickly, tears mingling with her whispers.

"You're the only one to have seen me," she was saying to me. The man you saw is dreadfully jealous. He knows that neither his fortune nor his threats can make me love him. He's very rich, and besides he knows a secret which gives him the power to keep me not only deaf, dumb and blind as soon as I'm amongst strangers, but also to make me invisible to them and to make me disappear into thin air. You caught me once when the sun's slanting rays deflected my companion's power. Make sure you avoid his wrath. In the early mornings, when he goes off to the spa, he locks me in but allows me to remain visible. Go away now, for he'll soon be back, but try to think of a way of get me out of this situation."

I heard steps on the stairs and slipped away. I returned to my room, shocked. I had made up my mind! I would wait for the next day, and then I would force the door and carry off the unknown woman.

All sorts of thoughts of heroism prevented my enjoying the beautiful alpine scenery that morning. I went into the dining room early and, taking advantage of the absence of the waitresses, I placed the chair opposite the one where Mr. Impavidus would be sitting in such a way that it was bathed in the light coming slanting through the window. Those few words from the unfortunate young woman had been enough to allow my imagination to reconstruct her miserable existence. I could see that she was treated like a slave by her pompous companion. Carrying out all his activities methodically, even at the most harrowing or the most blissful moments, taking away the visibility of the young woman or restoring it to her, kissing her hands or her lips with kisses calculated and measured like chemical formulae, preventing her seeing and being seen, removing her from the world for whose pleasure she had been created; I could see him, this old sorcerer (magic had not been able defeat his baldness nor the folds of fat on his cheeks and the nape of his neck), I could see him reducing everything to fit in with his wishes. He dominated the adorable being who had fallen under his control. He riled her with his self-importance and the high opinion he had of himself. He must have rolled his eyes when he spoke to her. He must have taken her for a fool, for someone inferior to himself, for a lower order.

He imposed his presence on her all day long, dragging her into the small canoe, placing himself not only between her and the rest of humanity, but also between her and the horizon, between her and the water.

I had at all costs to give this young woman back her life and liberty.

The dining room had filled up and the waitresses were already moving around with dishes of food. Mr. Impavidus's place was still empty.

Towards the end of the meal I could bear it no longer and I spoke to the waitress.

"He's late then, the gentleman over there in the corner?"

"He's left the hotel," came the reply and I thought my heart was going to stop.

I ran to the reception desk where I learned that Mr. Impavidus had indeed, early that morning on coming back from the spa, settled up and left.

"Besides," added the clerk, looking at me suspiciously, "Mr. Impavidus complained that you had got the wrong room this morning and that you had disturbed him."

"Not this morning," I answered, "yesterday evening."

"No, no," replied the clerk, irritated, "it was this morning around seven o'clock, according to Mr. Impavidus. He seemed very angry."

Ashamed, I went away. So Mr. Impavidus knew I'd been in touch with the young woman. And he'd rushed away. No one at the hotel could tell me which city he lived in.

I spent the rest of my holiday full of sadness.

When I got back to the Bank I was called into the office of the head of personnel:

"We're letting you go, permanently and irrevocably," he told me. And he handed me an envelope with a month's pay. I protested, and finally got an appointment to see one of the directors.

"I can't do anything about it," he said to me. "It was Mr. Impavidus's decision."

"Mr. Impavidus?"

"Yes, our new managing director."

Since that day it has been impossible for me to find work. I have made sure not to tell the story of Mr. Impavidus for he has a lot of power and after taking away my daily bread he could take away my very soul.

All that remains for me to do is wander around the streets, dream in the parks and wait for Mr. Impavidus to forget about his vengeance.

Then a man aged around forty joined us. He looked so like me that I wondered if I had become the plaything of a malevolent duplication. He began speaking as follows:

One day when I shall be least expecting it I shall have the actions of my whole life explained to me. I shall be present, outside myself, looking in at everything I have been and done. I shall see my childhood self amongst other children, looking through a window at a boat hoisting its sails. As a young man, later on, on the deck of a ship, not as huge as the one he carries in his heart. In a chilly town, running through the streets one morning to knock at the dark door of his workplace. Yes, I did that. And the other one too. I have been that man walking along the edge of a lake, his gaze lost amongst the clouds. I have been the deaf and dumb man, holding in his arms the love of his life and trying to get his tongue around words heavier than stones. In the midst of the crowd, this young bird seller. I shall see all that. I shall be the unsatisfied man. The loner. The person carried away by easy success. The unconsoled. And the happy man. And the sad man. And suddenly I shall be told (and the voice will be closer to me than myself) this is the action that has got you committed. It will be a very simple action, without any obvious significance, like opening a door or the shutters at a window, or going into a shoemaker's small workshop with a pair of shoes for repair tucked under my arm. And I shall be amazed: how could I have known? That man I considered to be my friend had the skin of his face scraped off; without it you could see his veins and all the hate spurting from his bleeding flesh. Remember the station, where in the darkness you said your farewells to the woman you loved. The station's metallic clashing was all around and the woman walked away without turning her head. And suddenly you see: this woman is a she-wolf and she is surrounded by innumerable wolves, rubbing their fur against hers. See the woman abandoned in a darkness of the city which from time to time was lit up by searchlights combing the enemy's sky: here is a sea lion with its gentle and humble lament on a deserted beach. How could I have suspected it? Now here I am in a brightly lit hall where a crowd of dancers spin to the rhythm of an orchestra. The woman watches me with her unforgettable gaze.

And suddenly I am changed into a pig.

Yes, it's a pig now dying on the shining floor of that hall. And this pig is me.

And I don't know that I'm a pig and all those around me don't know it either. Except the dark-haired witch laughing, her mouth wide open. I'm overwhelmed with an infinite sadness. Now I'm wallowing in mud and enjoying the freshness coming through my rough skin. Here I am, unsettled by my appetites, displaying my small bloodshot and threatening eyes. This vision hangs around for too long. I'm going to shake myself, drag myself from the filth. But now what do I see? I'm really this pig, resisting with all its strength as they try to drag it to the slaughterhouse door. It's in a well-populated district in the south east of the capital city. Children are laughing, men stopping to watch me without pity. Young couples walking along with their arms around each other. Ah! Who will save me from my fate? You alone, woman, could save me if you were compassionate. But you turn your face away. And now, a few more steps, and the tall gloomy doors of the slaughterhouse are opening. I pull so hard on the rope that it's strangling me. Enough, enough, I cry and I cover my eyes. But now what's happening? With my eyes closed and covered up I can still see. I can see the whole of myself. I am the vision and the visionary.

This scene is never-ending! You, kindly woman, wife or mother, are turning your head towards me. You're crying out in horror. "Stop! The one you're dragging along is a man." You touch my forehead with your gentle hands and here I am standing on my feet and resuming my human appearance.

I'm weeping with joy and I start up a song of gratitude:

What was I before you bestowed your gaze on me?
A beast on its knees being stalked in the street
You alone recognised my haggard face
My body lied to you, but you believed my soul.

May you be blessed for your welcome to me, and my wounds
Are healing like a bird amid the flock
You make the ground firmer beneath my feet
You place your cool hands upon my burning brow.

Your wondering eyes have also touched the town
Like two smooth pebbles on the lake's surface
And all is beautified; the street, so hostile yesterday
Is tracing the lines of your veins.

May you be praised, for as I came near
You did not turn away in horror
Like the stream beneath the dry rock
You divined my beauty beneath my ugliness.

And you understood my pain and my sadness
The song imprisoned in my grunts
You cried out "An end to this sorcery"
And my blood raced joyfully in my breast.

As an honour to the restored man, and at table
You placed me on the side of your heart
Even my shadow had fled the pigsty
You silenced the evil ones and the mockers.

Far away the sorceress uttered blasphemies
For you had spoiled all her fun
And my face lights up and loves you
Your eyes have brought it back to life.

When the author of this poem stopped speaking the great figures of night came towards us. They were silent beasts with a sliver of stars on their muzzles. Buffalos with muddy, cracked skin like the earth in a drought were moving around heavily, darkly. I found myself surrounded by vast marshes teeming with a strange world of pieces of night and birds growing slowly larger like oil slicks. The old man, the char-woman, the out of work lover, the poet had all disappeared. I was alone now before the shifting dark shadows which, not knowing they were watched, were taking it easy, letting their desires run free. I could see them, like large clouds, scarcely living things, bumping into one another, shifting around in the empty silence. They were playing like this with a grave and serious mien. I could feel their breath on my face. The night had become an enormous stable. "I am hunger," cried one of them. "I am thirst," cried another. "I am despair," announced a third. And saying that they hopped from right to left, enjoying themselves no doubt, captivated. It was their way of dancing. It was a family reunion. "I am disaster," cried a shape even more enigmatic than the others. War, poverty made their entrance and the muffled rumbling of thunder was heard. My eyes were getting used to distinguishing the shadowy shapes. It was the hour at which a large part of the world slides into sleep's abyss. That which vision circumscribes and limits is suddenly freed, flowing and fleeing everywhere. Night is the saucepan left forgotten on the fire, the milk swelling up and overflowing. Long serpents slide out of holes in tree trunks hissing loudly: "We are calamities, we are epidemics, grief."

"I am here" cried cruelty. Ingratitude, adultery were slithering, cold and slimy, along the ground. Indistinct shapes were scarcely perceptible as they glided along. Rats were emerging all over the place, jackals, hyenas, wild cats. Treachery, scornfulness, presumption, selfishness were mixing with these venomous droves. Gradually the despair which had taken hold of me abated. Then I had an urgent desire to tame these creatures, to subdue unhappiness and darkness, to bind them with strong ropes and lead them, submissive and docile, into the town. I could picture myself arriving one morning at the edge of town. Where they have the horse markets. Behind the houses, you suddenly find squares, covered in incomprehensible stakes and markers, where groups of men are gathering, apparently for something very serious. I remember that cattle market I had discovered on Sunday when I was a child. My family had moved to the capital shortly before. That Sunday my brother who was four years older than me (he was fourteen) took me early in the morning for a walk in town. Leaving the centre we mistook the way and went in the opposite direction to the one leading home. And suddenly we found ourselves at the edge of a square full of carts laden with hay, with impatient horses and countryfolk. Townspeople with a preoccupied look were moving to right and left amongst them, stopping amid the groups, leaning over the horses' rumps. My brother and I, stunned speechless, watched these mysterious comings and goings, these horse dealers with their broad shoulders, their hats pushed back, their loud voices and laughter. The crowd was spreading all around among the stakes. Animals waited their turn at the drinking trough. We stayed there a long time, dazzled by this spectacle. It was only very late, in the evening, that we found the right way back home. Our parents, to whom we described our adventure, nodded incredulously. "Who knows what misdeeds you have on your conscience," father said to us. We ate our dinner in tears. I for a long time afterwards, not being able to get to sleep, tried to understand why my father had doubted that we had got lost in the cattle market district. But for a long time the shadowy forms of the horses and carts around the water fountain, the horse dealers, the countryfolk, the buyers, the sellers and the massive figure of the presiding vet haunted my sleep.

And now here I was arriving amid the crowd with my drove of dark shadowy figures, with the black buffaloes of hatred, the gloomy hippopotamuses of sadness, the stormy clouds of despair. I shall take them on, I shall conquer them, I shall lead them defeated through the city streets. "What are these creatures?" people will ask. And the children, the women, the gawpers will come running. Space will be cleared in the markets. People will appear at the windows, others will stay on their doorsteps. And I, with my hair blowing around, my face tanned by the fires of night and the salt of tempests, I shall shout to them:

"Get some big sites ready, surrounded by high grilles and impregnable walls. For here come famine, war, spoliation, lies, acts of oppression, master's insolence, dishonesty, deception sharing, monopolies, enrichment to the detriment of others, poverty, unhealthy existence, shoddy work, and plenty of other monsters that I have defeated and bring here to captivity. Prepare vast camps for these monsters. They are not for sale. Do not open the doors of your markets. We shall lock them in the marshy part of town. They must be watched. For I don't know how long I shall be able to keep them in my power. Light joyful bonfires to celebrate this day, for henceforth there will be neither suffering, nor separation, nor abandonment, nor drought. And he amongst you who will try to take over these monsters and use them to take advantage of his fellow men, he will be burnt at the stake. Anyone who tried to bribe the sentries and slips into the park at night to learn how to take charge of these creatures will be fed to them.

"Let the humble ones, those who have nothing, those thirsting after peace and quiet, let them rise up and come to bear witness. Let the column of the brightest dawn be erected. The day, feeling so joyous, gives off a perfume of an apricot tree in blossom. The rivers are like spindles, from which the great tapestries of the ocean are woven. And on Sundays, for a modest sum in the garden of monsters, people can see stretched out in their cages Hatred, Greed, Despotism, Vengeance and so many other creatures once so evil and controlled by a powerful force."

⁂

I was astonished to see it was daylight. I was sitting on the same bench. The square was rapidly lighting up. To start with it was the voices of the early morning vendors: announcing the first newspapers, the fresh bread rolls, the milk curds. There were clear sounds too: market gardeners' horses trotting by, the jingling of the milk-men's carts, the footsteps on the shining pavements of those who, rising before dawn, were going to meet their destiny. I have often thought that you can tell whether it's night or day by listening to sounds. Nor is the silence the same. Like the blind man who can recognise and name things by using his fingers, you must be able just by listening to noises say whether it's morning or evening, whether it's raining or fine, if you're in the mountains or at the seaside.

So with my eyes still blurred with sleep I realised that day had broken. Standing leaning over me was the old man, whom I had forgotten amongst all the other happenings of the night.

"You're still there?" I asked, startled.

"Of course my friend," he replied.

His eyes were brighter now. You would have thought that the dawn had washed away the wrinkles from his face. "I won't leave you until I've shown you round the town." He drew his hand from the pocket of his big overcoat and showed me a large key. I immediately thought that this old man was in charge of an old church. We had arrived at the park gates and the street ahead of us was open to us. "This key," the old man answered my thought, "is not as you believe intended to open an ancient dwelling. Take hold of it; of course, it's a key like any other key, a little bigger, a little more rusty, perhaps heavier. It's a key which has been passed down in my family from father to son. It came from a great-grandfather who was a famous locksmith. It is the key to reality."

We had arrived in a noisy street where dense crowds were rushing around on all sides. A beautiful day was beginning and clearly the town dwellers wanted to make the most of it before the forthcoming bad weather season. The shops were full of people. The sun was climbing quickly up into the sky in order to watch the city's joyful bustle. I was seeing again houses that had witnessed my childhood and my early youthfulness, so I had known their walls for a long time. Leading away from the centre with its statue of one of the town's great men were avenues and boulevards lined with luxurious mansions. "I know all of this town," I could not help exclaiming. "What new do you want to show me?" "Have a little patience," replied the old man.

At the end of the avenue was the town's most glorious residence. I had passed by it hundreds of times with a feeling of respect. In front of its entrance two large marble lions seemed to be guarding the great door. On party evenings dazzling light would be thrown from the ruby-encrusted windows. In the courtyard, surrounded with great vases of exotic flowers, fine carriages with horses pawing the ground and coachmen dressed like generals would usually be waiting. "Follow me," said the old man, and he began to climb up the enormous stone staircase. The door opened as if by magic and we found ourselves in an immense hall with colonnades of porphyry, where precious stones and furniture and golden amphora gleamed. It must have been lunch time, for a great table setup in the middle was laden with plates of fruit and mouth-watering dishes. Seated around the table in tall velvet armchairs gentlemen and ladies of the high nobility were calmly and pleasantly conversing. I looked at my shabby clothes and I heard the old man whisper to me: "Don't worry! No one will pay any attention to you. These people are too full of themselves, of their own happiness, to notice us." I recognised in the place of honour the town's most eminent man. His breast shone with medals. He was surrounded by beautiful and elegant young women and smartly dressed and courteous men. Liveried servants with serious expressions circulated to right and left, laden with salvers. At the far end of the hall an orchestra was playing quietly. Scraps of phrases detached themselves from the music and hovered in the air. There was an atmosphere of happiness, riches, well-being, love, journeys, promenades, encounters.

How many times had I, when young, dreamed of being admitted to this place of blissfulness. I used to walk past the walls of this mansion; I would imagine the parties happening inside, the couples dancing happily there. But entry was reserved for the upper classes. I could have got inside there as a servant. But even amongst servants there was also an elite class which I could not aspire to. I had to be satisfied with admiring from afar these premises, so captivating in my imagination.

And today the old man that chance had brought to meet me in the square had made the doors of this palace open.

The people, immersed in their bliss, gave no sign of having noticed our presence. Of course, they couldn't see us for they were too absorbed in their pleasure. I followed the old man's light steps. The silks, the marbles, the beautiful dresses, the harmonious voices, the faces with their expressions of joy and goodness almost made me dizzy. I became wrapped up in this easy lifestyle. I could feel that I was no longer able to distinguish between me and these people; that I myself must have a happy face. Had the brilliance of their clothes not transferred to mine? Hunger, cold, sadness were far away. You see, I was telling myself, it's enough for their doors to be opened to feel welcomed and loved as they are. A maître d' stopped in front of me and offered me a glass of champagne. "Take it," the old man said to me, and he too took a glass. Everyone here was trying hard to be kind to their neighbours. The orchestra stuck up a hymn and they all got to their feet and toasted each other courteously. Oh! I was experiencing again the ecstasy I had felt as a child when I would glue my forehead to shop windows full of wonderful toys. But this time I was inside the window; I was enjoying the flames of a distant sky. I had already forgotten the presence of the old man when he touched my shoulder and gestured to me to follow him. We made our way towards the back of the room and stopped in front of a high and imposing door. Looking back, I saw with amazement that the table and the friendly guests were further away than the short space we had crossed would indicate. I could still see them, with their smiling faces, but their voices scarcely reached my ears. Like this, it was an even more impressive sight. The multicoloured dresses mingling with the men's dark attire, the gentle and friendly gestures: even seated these people looked as if they were taking part in a courtly and joyful dance. So where was the old man taking me? What other room was hiding behind this cold door? My guide had taken out the large key and was leaning over the lock. Then I heard the grinding of iron and groaning of the hinges. I looked back once again as if to bid farewell to the happy crowd. But a blast of cold air had blown in through the half-open door. First I saw leaves and napkins flying off the tables, then the light dimmed. I looked as hard as I could: crevasses and dust covered the colonnades, the walls. The room, so beautiful a few moments before was nothing but a hovel in ruins. I ran back to the table. The guests, as if they were the playthings of some evil sorcerer, were now dressed in rags, their faces aged and sad. Where the beautiful young women had been there were now only old beggar women. The medals had disappeared and amid the great disorder the remains of some disgusting meal were piled up. The voices were hoarse and the looks full of hatred. Some men had started a quarrel and were exchanging insults. In a corner three men were savagely tearing apart a woman whose cries were lost amid the general uproar. Nothing any longer indicated that here there had been friendly beings full of beauty and goodness. You would have said that the amiable faces had been swept away like masks by the wind, to be replaced by evil and repulsive faces. Anguished, I asked the old man: "What's happening?"

"Come," he replied, and he dragged me outside. I looked at the façade of the beautiful mansion. It was now a cottage with peeling walls. All the splendour I had so lusted after had disappeared.

The daylight had dimmed and back in the street we found it dismal and silent. The old man walked along wordlessly. Soon we left the town centre and entered an outlying district. Everywhere were small makeshift hovels. Night was fast falling and clouds were covering the sky. A little bare foot girl was carrying two buckets of water. This child gave off a great feeling of sadness, dragging herself along, bowed down with the weight. She was making for a small wooden hut surrounded by bits of scrap iron, the remains of broken barrels and stacks of rubbish. "Can't I help you, little girl?" I asked her; but she looked at me fearfully, almost with hostility. "What's the point," she replied, "I do this job several times a day. You won't always be there to help me. We're lucky to have a water fountain in the street." What the child called a street was no more than a muddy path lined with makeshift shelters. She allowed me to take one bucket, the old man took the other and we followed her into the hut. Here reigned disorder and filth. Rags and disparate objects were piled up in the middle of the narrow room. Five children of various ages got tangled up in our legs. They made faces and shouted insults at us. Their mother, fat and ugly and wrapped in a ragged shawl, threw herself between them, slapping their faces. A man with a beard and a miserable look who seemed to be busy repairing a mattress shouted to us by way greeting: "Put the buckets behind the door. You shouldn't get the child into lazy habits. She'll pay for it later." The little girl who seemed to be the eldest started silently laying the table. She put out plates and wooden spoons on the stained tablecloth. The man, who had got up from his work covered in dust, said to us in the same grumpy voice: "Stay with us. You can share our meagre dinner." The old man indicated to me that we should accept and we squeezed around the table. The air was suffocatingly stuffy between the unmade beds, the disembowelled mattresses, the stove on which a large stew pot was simmering. The children were shouting, crying, banging on the table. The mother went from one to another, poking the fire in the stove, moving the chair. She served each one of us a bowl of soup in which cabbage leaves and turnips were floating. Everything was desolate here. No light, no hope. I made as if to eat, for I would not have liked to irritate these people. Their poverty, their crowded conditions, the meagreness of their meal made me feel ashamed. I felt responsible for their misery even though I had never had occasion to boast of my wealth. Indeed, I was just as poor as they were, and it would have been difficult to me to help them out. But I knew that their rough voices, their ill temper, their quarrelsome behaviour were simply a reflection of their pitiful situation.

The old man dragged me away from these thoughts. He had got to his feet and stammered a few apologies. He stepped over the bundle of rags and the bits of motheaten wool, jumped over overturned chairs and disappeared into the haze at the other end of the hovel. That was where I found him and it was as if I had journeyed through vast lands. Stretches of cloud had come between us and the dismal family. My heart was still heavy with the sadness of these people. The old man, as if preparing to open a door—although there was no sign of one—was holding in his hand the large key. With it he touched the wall of the hovel. A sudden beam of light then flooded into the premises. Each side of the room widened. Soft carpets stretched beneath our feet. The man and woman, their faces now beautiful and smiling, were chatting with their children who were dressed in velvet. They all looked happy and joyful. Through the large open windows came the scents of a fine garden. We could hear the birds singing. The table was laden with good things. I could not drag my eyes away from this comforting scene.

I sat down at the old man's side on a divan, far enough away from the amiable family not to intrude on their blissful intimacy.

"Could you tell me what happened?" I whispered to the old man.

"I've already told you," he began, "that one of my ancestors was a renowned locksmith. He was called to the wealthiest people to make keys and locks secretly. He would often see things that few mortal people can see. He had access to the most secure apartments. No one knew how to make more mysterious caskets than him, or to invent more impenetrable hiding places. Jewellery, precious stones, letters and parchments telling of love and hate passed through his hands. He knew about disputes, envies, vengeances. He would come away with a sense of sadness from the most joyful houses. In other apparently unhappy houses he would sometimes discover happiness. One of the richest men of his time asked him one day to make him a lock for his fabulous treasure. He worked for a long time on this lock. But when he had put it in place and tried to introduce the key into it a miracle happened. The precious objects, the bags stuffed with gold and silver started speaking and crying out, 'Don't lock us in here. We don't belong to this master. We belong to everybody.' And they named this one and that one of the rich man's fellow citizens from whom these things had been stolen. The voices became so loud that they reached the street, the whole town. The crowd heard them and invaded the corridors of the palace. Thus they all recognised the objects and the silver and gold which belonged to them. The thief, the embezzler of his fellow men, was dragged into a nearby wood and hanged. The treasure, redistributed, was now silent. The people thought that one of them had lent the objects his voice. Only my ancestor knew that the voices came from the objects themselves, awakened by the strange power of his key. He kept its burdensome secret. The key passed down from generation to generation of my family without losing anything of its power. Inserted into a lock, even a totally unfamiliar one, it conjured up the real character of a house.

"So you were able to see, like me, that beneath the luxury and harmony of the palace there was nothing but misery and ugliness. The countenances with their smiling appearance were just hiding visages of horror and profanity. The carpets, the valuable vases, the statues, the fountains scarcely covered up the peeling walls, the dilapidated furniture, the dark shadows of their souls. And those people engaging in polite conversation detested each other savagely. They look as if they want to exchange caresses but they're ready to throw themselves at each other, to tear each other apart, into small pieces. Face powder hides their wrinkles and their scowls. They offer drinks and refined dishes to each other but these are poisoned by their looks and their obscene thoughts.

"On the other hand, here, beneath the makeshift roof of this hovel is hidden the room of a real palace. These ragged beings, these sad children, are lords of beauty and love. They are beaten down and filthy, they hit each other, they hate life, and yet all it takes is the power of this key for their goodness and grace to appear.

"That is why this key is called the key to reality. Take your place amongst these happy people. Share their family meal. They have invited you." These were the old man's last words.

I sat down at the laden table close to the little girl whose bucket of water I had carried. Now she was wearing a beautiful silk dress and passing graciously from one to another of the guests. Laughter and light voices were echoing around the room. The mother was slicing up a large cake.

An aroma of happiness and tranquillity enveloped me. I did not want to miss a single moment of this evening's party. Finally, I was saying to myself, here I am in the midst of a welcoming and happy family. Perhaps they'll adopt me as one of their own. The father got to his feet. I admired the perfect cut of his jacket, his carefully trimmed beard detracting in no way from his handsome face.

"My children," he said, throwing a malicious glance in my direction, "I am going to tell you a wonderful story. You must all listen, it's the story of the key to reality."

WHAT'S IT ALL FOR?

For Léon-Gabriel Gros[1]

I admired that street vendor in the square of a provincial town whose name I have forgotten who spoke thus to an elderly lady who had just joined the group surrounding him: "Good day, madam, I apologise for not welcoming you as I should have done; I was busy with a client. Otherwise it would have been a pleasure to open the door for you myself." And dismissing with a gesture an imaginary person: "You can go, young man, I will look after madam. Do come in please." And he bowed low. The people listening smiled happily. The elderly lady seemed entranced, and she looked younger. A charmed atmosphere surrounded the street vendor. If he had been an important merchant at the entrance to a splendid palace this setting would not have seemed more attractive. I myself saw the great doorway, the sales assistants busily setting out the packages of merchandise, the crowd of gentlemen and elegant ladies

1 Léon-Gabriel Gros (1905-1985), French poet and critic.

going from counter to counter to make their choices. They were all there, listening to the clever vendor who, whilst speaking quickly, forgot none of the rules of politeness, of careful diction and of brilliant expressions. Passers-by were stopping; they swelled the ranks of spectators, they put aside indifference and weariness to allow themselves to be charmed by the splendour of some object that, without the vendor's magic touch, would not have provoked any longing or any desire. Perhaps his hands were empty? Perhaps they held neither the illusory laces of shoes which he claimed he would sell off before a sudden departure, nor the braces which according to him were a special bargain. His words were enough to intoxicate us all and we would have gladly opened the secret purses of our souls. As I left him I remembered the work places, the offices, the stations, the factories, the hospitals scattered across the years of my life. Are all these buildings more real than the imaginary palace of the street vendor? Is it not rather our constant fear of seeing the world we rush about in fade away that pushes us to invent rules, archives, deeds of ownership or of sales, registers of accounts and official documents? Suddenly I envisage those huge ugly buildings where innumerable employees work. Hundreds of thousands of employees. A room where men and women hunched over sheets of paper draw diagrams, note figures. Further on dossiers are set up, piled one on top of the other in shiny boxes. In another room contracts, letters, invoices, transfer orders are being typed. But what's it all for, in the end? Ask the first person you come across, the doorman who opens his boss's door. What's it all for? With a ceremonial smile the second-in-command will tell you, "Ask the head of department." After keeping you waiting for a while the latter can't tell you any more than his second-in-command. "Ask to speak to the director," he'll tell you in the end. Neither the director, the head of administration nor the chairman of the board will have an answer for you. Someone, decades ago, started this work one day. He recruited a colleague, he started putting files together, registering names, addresses, sums to be paid out or paid in; then others came to join in. They created the medical department, the property buying department, the mortgage department, the insurance policy department, the disaster department, the printing department, the cancellation department, the loan department, and when all these departments were fully occupied they invented others: the files department, the transformations department, the food provision department, the backdated premiums department, the pro rata department, the discount department . . . this department and that department, and each person is at their post, and every morning the offices fill up with noisy young people sitting at typewriters, calculators, or franking machines. Each one getting on with their work, of course . . . Look, here's the dossiers department. I watch the head of the department who proudly shows me that perfection of his system. "Fine," I say to him, "but do you know that the people whose names are shown here don't exist? And these dossiers,

Mr Chief Archivist, concern matters which have never existed?" I see the eyes of those I'm speaking to widen, fear takes hold of them. Pointless to frighten them I tell myself. "I was joking. Get back to your desks. Carry on working." It's better if no one knows what it's all for. And years pass like this: the typists type letters, the archivists set up their dossiers and their charts for estates, people, buildings which don't exist anywhere. Besides, who would care whether all that exists or not. They write the names, the figures, they do additions, they balance the books, all that works, it's perfect, the offices are full of people. If one of the employees leaves, a new one replaces him straight away. And so the years go by. They are all so used to making their gestures, compiling their lists, setting up invoices and birth and death certificates, that if one day someone removed the walls, the tables, the cupboards from these places, they would not notice. They would continue to see them in place as if nothing had happened. Besides, how would they not continue to see them, since all these things are imaginary? In the mornings they open imaginary doors, they sit at imaginary tables, they work on imaginary dossiers concerned with people who have never existed. And they themselves, do they exist? And the street vendor who opened an unreal door, was he less unreal than that door? Suddenly I'm far away, I can no longer hear the noise of those machines, no newspaper seller is proclaiming sensational news. I'm on a bench in a deserted park, it's evening already, night will soon come to spread its balm upon the wounds of the day.

No one is waiting for me. And darkness will wipe away my traces without anyone realising that my shape is no longer detectable in the air and without knowing that shortly before I had been slumped there, in the twilight, asking myself and without having the answer, "What's it all for?"

A LITTLE ORDER

For Gabriel Bertin[1]

"You leave your things lying around on your desk," the head of department often said to me as he sat opposite. "Before you go home in the evening you should put your papers away."

On other occasions the boss would just throw me an almost spine-chilling look. He didn't keep rebuking me but his glance said it all. All around me letters, files, accounts, receipted invoices piled up more and more. The drawers were full of them. Amongst the dust which covered the desk, shabby from years of work and wear, I would sometimes find a note with a long-past date reminding me of a distant event of my youth. "I must put away all these letters, make the desk clean and tidy," I would often say to myself. But the days went by, other urgent tasks claimed my attention and I never managed to tear away the thick spider's web of disorder.

1 Gabriel Bertin (1896-1945), French poet

One evening when the other staff had already left and I was ploughing through an interminable addition the boss, who for some time had seemed no longer bothered about my mess, suddenly said to me, indicating the desk: "God knows what I would find if I looked into this indescribable mess." It was a rainy late summer evening. The rain splashing the open windows did not lessen the heat of the room. The light shone weakly through the dusty lampshades. A thick silence like a stream of glue circulated between inside and outside. The tall form of the boss now loomed beside me and, humiliated and distressed, I looked at the pile of papers and files lying on the desk.

"Why are you keeping all these? Haven't I told you that the files have to be put back in their places?"

He had a malicious look in his eye. It was as if he took pleasure in reminding me of my shame and my faults. I remained sitting in my chair, my head bowed, arms hanging loosely.

"Let's have a little look," added the boss, and bending suddenly he opened the middle drawer.

The movement was so unexpected that I was almost knocked over backwards. And to my amazement the boss pulled out of the drawer a horse, the size of a toy at first, but which, as soon as it was put down on the floor, grew to normal size. It filled the room, pawed the ground and kicked its legs; it shook its mane and bumped into desks and chairs.

"Well, well!" exclaimed the boss, "That takes the biscuit."

He turned his back to the horse and his wicked smile brightened his face.

"Let's have another look," and he opened the right-hand drawer.

Immediately a tree appeared. Its roots dug into the floor, its trunk with its powerful branches rose and pierced the ceiling.

"Did you think about the damage?"

I tried to murmur an apology but nothing coherent emerged. I had recognised the tree. It was my favourite, growing in front of the steps of my childhood home in the countryside. Just as in the past, the birds were making their racket among the leaves. They must have been frightened by their sudden exposure. The light from the lamps, although feeble, had interrupted their sleep. Could I have suspected that this beloved tree, into whose shade I would sometimes escape in my memory, could I have suspected that it was there, within reach of my hand, amongst the business letters, amongst the bailiffs' and lawyers' files?

"I assure you I knew nothing about it," I finally managed to come out with.

The look on the boss's face gave me to understand that he didn't believe a word.

The horse had settled down at the foot of the tree. I recognised him too. It was the one I had mounted at the age of fourteen, proudly setting off down the little street where a teenage girl my age, who I was madly in love with, lived. I had picked this horse from the stable of the forest management company where my father worked as an engineer at the time. It was the eve of my departure for the city where I was to be lodged whilst at school. I passed in front of the girl's house several times; the window was not opened, but I detected a trembling of the curtain from behind which the loved one must have been watching. The next day I left for the city.

⁂

Since then I have moved to new pastures, new dreams, another climate. And now it seemed that the horse of my youthful hubris had followed me. I went up to him and stroked his nervous neck. His mane trembled like water in the breeze. The leaves of the tree were singing. I reached for a branch and with a flexibility I thought I was no longer capable of I climbed up onto it. The windows had disappeared into the distance, the street and its rainy light had vanished behind a haze.

"I don't want any more of this stuff," the boss said to me. "This isn't a stable. It's not a field."

Perhaps it was fear that made me climb higher. I had now reached the topmost branches. The boss's voice was becoming fainter and fainter. I looked down at him and realised he was getting smaller as I watched. Now he was hardly as big as my hand.

"It's the height of carelessness," he cried, but I could hardly hear him.

Soon he'd disappeared from view. I was high up in the tree, near its top, the wind murmuring around me and the night exuding its scented breaths. The birds, so scared to start with, finally came and perched on the branches around me. It was a really blissful few hours!

The next day my desk was in perfect order.

"You see, it's possible to get some order into it," the boss said to me, with a wink.

Taking advantage of a moment when he'd gone out of the room I opened the drawers, intrigued; an odour of resin was given off, but all the papers were in good order. Feeling something cold, I drew out my hand. I was holding a horseshoe and it was with this in my hand that the boss found me when he came back.

"Now what, a horseshoe!" the boss said to me. "That can bring good luck. But still you're not going to go in search of the horse that lost it."

And as if to show me that a little disorder didn't bother him, he put the horseshoe down amongst the files on the desk.

"It will make an excellent paper-weight."

MY ROOM

For Pierre Barbier

A path runs through the middle of my room. Yes, a path crosses my bedroom. My bed is between two doors, and these two doors are connected by a path. I also have a window. The window and one of the doors open onto a terrace on the fourth floor of an old block of flats. This terrace is wide enough to contain a small garden, a few shrubs, a henhouse and a rabbit hutch. The other door opens onto the landing of a wide staircase. The terrace faces south. The door to the staircase is on the north side. My bed is against the west wall. On the east side, at the bottom of an empty wall, is a small table with books and manuscripts.

It was only after I'd been living there for a few weeks that I noticed that a path crossed my room. To start with, when I came back from town with my shopping,

I would sometimes find a few blades of grass or bits of vegetables on the floor. But without stopping to work out where these scraps came from I would plunge into my reading or else stretch out on my bed to daydream, with my gaze fixed far above my head, my eyes like two little smoke circles rising up to the ceiling. Certainly, the path was hidden in the crevices of the wooden floor and only showed up when I wasn't there. But gradually, as it got used to my movements and my voice, it started to come out of its hiding place. One evening when I had come home earlier than usual and was lying on my bed taking advantage of the last hours of daylight to read a poem from times past, the door to the staircase opened suddenly and a large woman rushed across my bedroom, her arms full of greens, and went out of the door onto the terrace. I could hear her out there moving boards around, and saying two or three times: "Oh! The little devils!"; then she returned the way she had come without paying any attention to me; I realised afterwards that it was one of my neighbours bringing food for the rabbits on the terrace. Both doors were now open. And like a sort of quarter moon appearing from behind the clouds the little path showed up faintly. Shortly afterwards the large woman and a smaller woman, accompanied by a little girl, came through my room, without seeing me. or at least without looking at me. The woman who must have been the little girl's mother was carrying peas in her apron. "We must hurry," the woman was saying. "It's time to plant the peas."

⁂

From that evening onwards the path was no longer afraid to show itself; it became completely visible, resplendent with its small pebbles in the starlight. Every day, lying on my bed, I would see women and children passing along it, going from the darkness of the house to the terrace gardens. Young men, with a book or notepad under their arm, would also walk through my room and disappear, dreaming or chatting, into the alleyways of the terrace. Looking out of the window I saw that this terrace had become almost as big as a park. Little rabbits which had escaped from the hutch were running around or playing along the paths. Fearless, they would go up to visitors, or else they would sit up on their hind legs and beg, waving—and smiling, you would have said—their front legs. Hens were pecking contentedly around the shrubs. My bedroom path was in full flight; increasing in boldness it revealed itself completely without fear of surprising or annoying me. It was a lovely little path, with a romantic tint by the light of the moon. But even in daylight the path did not hesitate to show itself in my room. There was no more reticence. There was a continual coming and going between the doors, now for bringing food for the animals, now to hang out the washing, now to call to someone in the street below, now just to take the air or to breathe the scent of the roses in bloom on the terrace. Who would have worried about my presence, who would even have thought about it? Of course, my work, my reading suffered from it all. I no longer felt at home, I was living in the middle of a road; for the path had grown, it was doing really well, it was spacious and airy between the two doors which now stayed open. One evening I heard a tinkling of little bells, the swish of whips, the neighing of horses. Through the door from the terrace a wagon full of greenery was coming along the path of my room. On it young girls and young men were laughing and singing. The horses reared up for a moment in the middle of my room and then they vanished through the door leading to the staircase. But for a long time afterwards the air resonated with the laughter and the cracking of whips. The road, which to begin with had been no more than a small path connecting the terrace garden with the rest of the house, had become conscious now of its size and its strength. It was a wide avenue, happily carrying a carriage full of seasonal glories. My bed, getting smaller and smaller, huddled against the wall. After the wagon, groups of day trippers crossed my room. Then a wedding party passed by, and the horses pranced and the pistols cracked joyfully in the night air. By dawn the hustle and bustle on the road calmed down a little. A curious but timid rabbit came in through the terrace door and stopping in the middle of the road started watching me with its little red eyes. The road itself was amused by this tiny presence—after the night's major traffic. My eyes met the rabbit's. We were both strangers to the life and activities which were weaving around us. He was a prisoner of the hanging garden, I was living in a room which had been invaded by a path more and more like a river dragging everything along with it. And from one moment to the next I expected that my bed, the little table, the walls, the whole room would be carried away by the road which now stretched vigorously on both sides across the house and through the night, to disappear into the stars.

THE WOMAN AND HER DOUBLE

For André de Richaud[1]

It took me a certain amount of time to get used to the idea that the woman I loved was two people: one of them deep in my mind and the other separated from me by a barrier of foreign countries and mountains. I was not unaware that far away the woman I loved was popular and acclaimed. Men would bow as she passed, dressmakers, jewellers and flower-makers created corsages, finery and new gowns for her. So I was fearful that the image which had stayed with me of the one I adored would cut a sorry figure on the day when the real woman arrived to join her. "If they heap gifts and riches upon the distant woman," I said to myself, "I can do the same, if not better, for her double." Then I started dreaming of fabrics and royal gems. But as for cutting them and arranging them to suit the image in my mind, that was another matter. For I knew nothing of the dressmakers' and jewellers' art. And as for turn-

---

1 André de Richaud (1907-1968), French poet and writer.

ing to the professionals, there could be no question of it. They knew how to make gowns and finery for real women but would have no competence or knowledge of how to dress an imaginary being. Certainly, for me this intangible being was as real, if not more so, than her distant double. But aside from the fact that the dressmakers would have refused to work for an invisible body, the silks, diamonds and golds that I invented for my secret passion were so different from and superior to everyday materials that no one (except me) would have been capable of recognising them. Genuinely or not the craftsmen could even have claimed that these materials did not exist, and I could already envisage them exclaiming in indignation or mockery, "How do you expect us to make a gown out of nothing?"

So it would have been a waste of my time to count on outside assistance. Consequently I preferred to take a few dressmaking lessons myself and to this end I spent some time at one of the most famous workshops. But when I started putting together the luxurious invisible outfits I realised that the principles I had learnt were no use at all to me. The scissors and the needles used in the workshops had no effect on the best materials I had destined for the incomparable woman. I understood then that I had wasted precious days in trying to learn a profession which turned out to be of no use. During this time the far-away woman of whom I had only a mental image must have received more and more dazzling jewels and gowns. How to make up for the lost hours? How to fill up the wardrobes of my sweet vision with things as numerous and perfect as those received by the celebrated woman far away? Then, like a desperate man risking everything because he has nothing left to lose, I set about cutting the fabrics and the precious stones with no regard for the usual rules and norms. I worked until I dropped. And, like a blind man's fingers finding a piano's keys without the need for eyes, without the help of my eyesight I put together incomparable coats, blouses, shirts, bracelets, negligees. My work was in no way spoiled by my haste. The more I invented finery the more beautiful it was. I could laugh now at the alluring riches surrounding the distant woman. Her constant image alongside me was a thousand times more radiant, more decorative.

"Okay for the gowns," the real woman's followers seemed to be challenging me from afar, "but how will you manage for the gardens, the dwellings, the precious furnishings that we offer her? Admit that you're not up to competing with us." Not letting that put me off I set about making invisible furniture out of sycamore and ivory, plate glass palaces and temples which no eye could see, gardens with fountains and fairy lights. I had learned from the experience of being with the dressmaker. I knew now that it would have been a waste of time to learn the architect's profession. Without hesitation, and driven only by my passion, I built walls, I put up tree-lined avenues, I constructed arcades. Once a real green and splendid city was finished, I organised a gala in honour of the secret woman. No queen has ever known anything like it. Even the servants at this gala were better dressed, more noble and courteous than the kings and princes of the real thing. I myself stayed in a corner and watched the adored wraith looking for me amongst the dazzling throng. Her glance finally met mine. Oh! The gratitude, the goodness and the devotion I saw in it then.

"No, the real woman has never known such magnificence. Her image will never leave me for who could love and honour her more than I do?"

Proud and calmed by the success of this gala I made my way towards an isolated terrace like an arrogant host, smoking a cigar and withdrawing in order to savour his success and contemplate the crowd of his eminent guests. My glance slid towards the park gates beyond which the gawpers were gathering to catch a glimpse of the lights and colours of this happy gathering. And among these badly dressed and taciturn spectators imagine my astonishment at recognising the real woman whose adored image was the very centre point of the gala. She was watching wide-eyed and so absorbed in the wonderful scene that she did not even notice my presence, really close to her on the terrace. Her clothes were so meagre. A torn headscarf covered her beautiful hair. The only rings on her hands gripping the gates were their fever and impatience. Suddenly the adored woman seemed to shake her head, drag herself from the gates, and lose herself in the crowd. That was when I was aroused from my shocked state. I ran to the door, I pushed my way through the gaggle of gawpers, like a madman I called the name adored name, but the woman had disappeared. Where is she? How did she get back from her far country? I don't know. And now here I am, in despair and alone amongst the crowd watching the illuminations and the gala given for the unreal image of a woman I wasn't able to call to and keep with me in time. Here I am with my hair unkempt, my clothes dusty and torn, for I ran after the real woman, past the gate that the servants wouldn't allow me to come back in through. Unaware that they, as well as the garden, the palace, the dressed up guests and the finery of the unreal woman's double are nothing but an invention of my mind, these servants take me for a poor passer-by, they despise me and send me on my way.

CREATIVE GAMES

For Jean Rivier[1]

That morning, opening the window, I was seized with astonishment. Instead of the grey walls I had left there the previous day, an enchanting vista met my eyes. The pure air cleared my vision and filled my breast with happiness. I was already forgetting that I was in one of the city's sleazy districts. Beyond the leafy tops of trees rose the peaceful slopes of mountains. A halo of vapour trembled in the light of the rising sun. Upon the distant rocks I could see the brick roof tops of an abbey. I moved away from the window two or three times and came back to it with a beating heart, to discover to my delight that the beautiful vista was still there. So what had happened during the night? The window, narrow and low when I had left it, had become a large glazed door. I opened it and went onto the terrace, no longer in amazement. A gentle joy engulfed my soul. Where

1 Jean Rivier (1896-1987), French composer and Professor of Composition at the Paris Conservatoire 1948-66.

was I? For I was feeling the calm which had intoxicated me in a distant past. Something about this landscape belonged to a time when I was happy. Whether these dwellings and these trees existed or not was of little importance. They had perhaps emerged from my memories. I had thought of them so fervently that they had finally taken over reality. A young girl coming from the fountain stopped below the terrace and signalled to me with her hand. She was there as a witness. Leaning with my elbows on the balustrade I gazed for a long time at the glorious morning. Now the sun was spreading its shining mantle over the mountains. Regretfully, I dragged myself away from this vision. And I went down the dark stairs of my block to the road behind and made my way towards the city centre. I kept my eyes half closed so as not to allow the vision which had enchanted me during the morning to slip away. At the corner I took the tram, I went about my usual business and I was like someone constantly repeating a precious name or formula for fear of forgetting it. Towards the end of the afternoon I set off towards home: but already the shapes I had kept inside me all day had become more vague, less solid. When I got to my room I hastily opened the window. But no wonderful landscape appeared. There was a factory wall, the smoky street rising up a slope lined with old and dirty houses. I tried to remember the beautiful images glimpsed that morning. Where were the mountains now? No room, amongst the houses, for the green tree tops. No room in the distance either for the peaceful abbey roof tops. There I was like a child with the pieces of a jigsaw puzzle, not knowing where to put them. Nothing fits; certainly, I can remember the young girl at the fountain and the pines and chestnut trees and the slopes of the hills and the captivating horizon. But impossible to bring together all these disparate elements. I must have lost a piece of this beautiful puzzle when I was in the city. The light of day must have opened my eyes too far so that they dropped a vital piece. And I could not bring back between the walls of this dismal district the joy that had intoxicated me that morning. All I can do is shut myself in the room with a vague feeling of nostalgia, an indistinct yearning for a beautiful landscape of my childhood and holidays. Who knows, one day, opening the window, I might find it again. I could perhaps try to describe it in these pages, to find again its luminous entirety; but even as I write these words the vista slips away from me, it vanishes into the void, it returns to the dream from which it succeeded in escaping for a few moments one radiant May morning.

A PERMEABLE WORLD

For Jean Follin[1]

We are all permeable. Plants are permeable. Trees, stones are permeable. Animals are permeable. Men are permeable. I discovered this one sunny day when I was least expecting it. I was looking for a restaurant; I was dreadfully hungry for it was over twenty-four hours since my last meal. The restaurants I knew were closed. Notices at their doors said they could not open because of a shortage of foodstuffs. There was nothing to be had in that district. And it was as I was crossing the square from where the streets led towards the other side of the town that I made my discovery. A woman coming towards me suddenly appeared to me to be lying flat, like a large stain on the paving. An oil stain perhaps. There she was, stretched out, two-dimensional. Just her shape, no bulk. I could see her flattened body, her face spread over the paving, with a grimace of mixed hair and glances. It was too late to move back: I had already walked over her.

---

1 Jean Follin (1903-71), French author, poet and corporate lawyer.

It is possible that this was no more than an effect of hunger. My recent abstemiousness had made me excessively sensitive. I had lost a lot of weight, so that my senses no longer had to pass through the usual layers of fat and flesh to make contact with things. I had become as thin and delicate as an acoustic plate. All sounds, all vibrations were detectable. I had scarcely crossed the puddle which had been the elegant woman I had seen coming towards me when I noticed that I was walking through a gentleman; I was fighting my way through his middle, wrapped in him as if in a cloud of little midges or mosquitoes. He was quite a large gentleman, and it took me two or three seconds to go through him. But afterwards, as if I had been touched by one of the Graces, everything became understandable and visible. I easily passed through a tree. Then, through the inside of a horse. It was like a large patch of foliage shadow where the daylight quivered amongst the gaps in shade. I was so entranced by all this that I almost forgot my hunger. So every object, every being, was made of air. Standing, each one presented precise shapes and angles is if constituted of solid matter. But looked at from the side it was beyond doubt that they had only two dimensions. It was all on the surface, with no depth. That was why I had no difficulty moving through things and people.

Later I noticed some other surprising facts. I was moving through several beings at once. For example I was walking through a gentleman who (without his being aware of it) was moving through another gentleman or a lady, who in their turn were themselves moving through another person, who . . . etc., and I was moving through all of them at the same time. I would have liked to make some scientific observations as I experienced these strange processes. Was my heart beating more quickly? Was my blood richer or poorer in corpuscles? Was I borrowing something from the beings or objects I moved through or else was I giving them something of myself? To start with I had certainly had a dizzy feeling. But I was quite quickly getting used to that and now I moved with the grace of a skater. Were not beings or objects I was unaware of passing through me too? All this permeability perhaps results in a certain amount of incomprehension and disputes. If you get too close to someone you risk passing right through them, to the other side. All without realising it. There it is: one more step and you're behind and not in front of the person you want to talk to.—"What a rude person," they then exclaim. "Now he's turning his back on me. I'd have been better talking to a wall than to him."

And the walls! Are they permeable? Can you trust their separateness? Firstly, the least sensitive of men realises that sounds get through walls. And what is a sound? It is the transmission across distance of the sound of an object's or a being's shape. No one disputes that each sound corresponds to something characteristic and no one could take the clip-clop of a horse for the sound of a bell or an old gentleman's cough.

So with the sound of someone coming into your living quarters comes the person's shape itself, despite the walls all around. Vibrations in the air spread and multiply over a certain distance the contours of the source of the sound, without regard for obstacles, walls or trees, forests or hills. You can be comfortably settled at home, believing yourself to be protected from unwanted visitors and here come a thousand things, a thousand beings, penetrating the walls and setting upon you: it's a tram coming into your room and crossing through your permeable body and making all your limbs quiver; it's a concierge shouting at someone not to shake their carpets out of the window; it's a workman digging up the road with a pneumatic drill, and once he's made a hole in the pavement what does he find? Your very skin which the violent drill pierces. It's said that walls have ears. But they have eyes too. How can they be made deaf and blind?

This permeability of the air and of objects is the cause of several other of our troubles. Our inconstancy for example. We never know where a simple step might lead us. For we all wear seven-league boots. And no one can remove these boots. You might be amongst friends and pleasant people, laughing, dancing, and suddenly you take a step and you're far away and alone. That's because the seven-league boots have intervened. In this way you cross regions and landscapes, men and animals; suddenly you're in a foreign country, without hope and with no one to help you. So then you want to go back, find again what you have lost. But how: everything around us is permeable, our past is permeable, our present is permeable. You can't stop anywhere for you cross everywhere, you pass through everything. The step you take leads you elsewhere. Still further away. Our salvation would be to remove the permeability of objects.

Everything should be made opaque and hard. Scientists should be engrossed in this problem. Find a way to stop us passing through each other. So that we're no longer like a river bed over which the water flows carrying with it trees and sometimes even houses washed from the banks. For it is beyond doubt that everything flows through us. Yes, nature flows through us as through a sieve: through our eyes, through our sense of smell, through our ears, through our fingers, through our mouth; colours, perfumes, sounds, contours, the taste of the universe percolates through us unceasingly. Some of our senses are hungrier than others. Plants and animals get into us through our mouths. The world is a continual river, a waterfall flowing through our porous flesh. In this permeable world where everything penetrates every object and every object penetrates everything this constant circulation constitutes the very essence of life and death. Did I not, in order to become apparent and visible, first have to pass through my mother's flesh? From the nothingness where I was the powerful impulse of a will I was unaware of (for my will never intervenes in all these reasonings) propelled me towards the clay of which my mother was made. Passing through her (like an underground stream passing through a rock) I began to take shape, to gather consistency. But also like the underground stream washing away the qualities and the riches of the limestone, the iron or the salts of the rock it has passed through, I too carried away something of the virtues and the essence of my mother. That was quite a long journey, for it was the first I had undertaken in this world. But since then I have passed through beings, landscapes and objects at an increasing speed. My quivering face, only roughly sketched by a hesitant hand amongst the maternal light and shade, was later defined by the essence of this world I'm moving through and which in its turn moves through me.

I laugh now, when I think of the efforts made by municipalities to organise the circulation of people and traffic in their streets. Now you have to keep to the right. Now it's the left. Someone coming from one side has the priority, or someone coming from the other. The poor drivers don't know which way to look. They have to learn by heart the letter of the law and its interpretation. And the worthy man coming from his home in the morning to go to work must first study his route on a map. Some paths are prohibited, others you can take in the evening but must avoid in the full sun. In the big cities all that engenders such a nervous depression in some people that they give up going out altogether rather than having to study so carefully the pedestrian crossings, the pavements reserved for those going, or reserved for those returning, etc. . . .

The day when my discovery is recognised, how much simpler will moving around and journeys become! Why regulate traffic since we're all permeable. The trains, the lorries, the pedestrians will no longer have to avoid each other. They'll go through each other. Think of the beauty of two trains approaching each other. A few seconds still separating them. The drivers making desperate efforts to stop them. But it's as if two sides of a landscape were rushing towards each other. The mountains, the plains, the rivers are moving. There is huge joy in the air, a tremor hovering over the peaks and rumbling in the bowels of the earth. How could the feeble hands of men prevent this violent marriage? Finally the two trains meet and penetrate each other. One easily passes through the other. He who knows nothing sees afterwards only a heap of twisted metal and corpses. It's all a deception. The landscape has closed like a book with the trains as a bookmark between the pages. And the two convoys which have passed through each other continue their journeys across all the landscapes like a wedding procession. In the sky moons and suns pass through each other. On the seas, when two ships meet, they throw themselves upon and through each other, like the stars. And the water beneath them trembles with pleasure and makes waves as if two water lily leaves had fused together. The forests move upon the ground. They march towards one another, they mingle like two heads of hair or like the poles of two magnificent flags.

I'm in my bedroom now. The window looks out over a wide boulevard. I can see very clearly the trees climbing towards the peak of this landscape and the men moving around. Is that not a proof (if another were needed) of the interpretation of things? The window is two metres high and one metre wide. And the boulevard I'm looking at stretches along hundreds of metres. Dozens and dozens of men cross in front of the windowpane. They are all on this rectangle of glass: vehicles, people, houses, trees. It's the law of perspective, you'll say. Not at all! I'm not going to be taken in any more by these facile laws. Everything enters and pulsates and moves upon this windowpane, for everything is permeable. I have no longer any need to go somewhere else to pass through something or for something to pass through me. I'm sitting at this window, and the whole boulevard comes into my eye. It's like a tape measure wrapping itself around my pupil. Here is an exercise: I fix my eye on something as far away as possible, the top end of the boulevard; I watch for the arrival of someone walking, there he is. He is like a thread that I'm pushing through the needle of my gaze. He's approaching now, he's getting bigger. My eye doesn't leave him for a moment. And finally he disappears; he's entered my pupil, he continues on his way inside me, he passes through me and I don't know where he'll go afterwards. But for the moment he's inside me. I keep him safe, this nice person, with his grey slightly worn overcoat, his walking stick and his bowler hat. He can't be too old. Hardly forty. He had come from his office as usual to go to his restaurant. And this extraordinary adventure befalls him: he is the prisoner of my gaze. He must be a little frightened as he walks through my moist and dark tissue. Perhaps he's unaware that this glass pane covered with wet foam is the inside of my eye. What he takes for a crevice is a small scar on the side of my throat. Hey, watch out, you'll slip: now you're walking on my tongue. All these pathways seem unfamiliar to you. And you suddenly feel very alone. Don't let that bother you, my friend. I will find you a companion, man or woman. So I open my eyes and watch the boulevard carefully again. This man I took by chance. But woman I shall choose. The first who catches my eye is an old beggar woman. She drags her feet, with a bundle on her back. But does she have a foreboding? She has attached herself to my eyelids, to my eyelashes, she doesn't want to let go. She would perhaps be happy to walk around the inside of my eye. Somewhere, in an inhospitable and cold hovel, an ailing daughter and a feeble husband are waiting for her. Her life is a sad one, and her mouth forgot how to smile a long time ago. The unexpected prospect of a journey through a man would appeal to her, no doubt. But I think of the individual I have already inside me. This poor woman would just frighten him more. And finally I take my eye off her. And here in the window comes a young mother holding by the hand two little girls dressed in blue. The father, also young, is walking a little way behind them, reading a newspaper. It would be funny to make the mother and the two little girls disappear into my eye. The father, lifting his gaze over the newspaper, would be amazed to find himself alone. I can already see him rushing home, ready to remonstrate with the absent-minded young woman who wandered off with the little girls and who would certainly not arrive back until after him. But panic would soon take over from indignation. And I feel pity for the brave man; so I leave the woman and the two little girls with him and I see them all disappear down the bottom of the window pane, where it meets the wall. And the little group plunges into the wall and vanishes. Yet I need to find a woman. I exclude another one, a seller of peanuts and nougat who walks across the window pushing her little cart. Several schoolgirls pass, laughing so loudly that the whole window lights up. Finally there comes a young woman on her own, her supple bearing as she walks seeming to slide along the tightly stretched cord of my gaze. Now the window is like a violin and the woman is its bow. I shall let her move down the glass and only wrap her in my gaze shortly before she disappears into the wall. She walks dreamily, very slowly. I have time to see clearly her small black hat decorated with a feather which has nothing aggressive about it and which goes wonderfully well with her light and airy silhouette. Her black hair is loose and floats at the side of her face, its features still concealed from me but where I sense her hidden beauty. Beneath her little black suit, decorated with a white flower, a red blouse can be seen with its collar turned down. I am so moved by her grace that I almost forget to keep her back. But I remember in time, and just as she arrives at the edge of the glass pane where the spongy wall, thirsty for her fresh presence, is ready to snap her up, I lock her in my gaze and draw the heavy bolts of my eyelids. There, now she's inside me.

I'm already thinking about the joy of the solitary gentleman when he sees her appear. Now let's see, I shall need to make the landscape inside me more cheerful. At the far end of the avenue the contours of the mountains are outlined against the sky. Beyond them glistens the sea. And like a gambler gathering up bundles of bank notes from the gaming table and stuffing them in his pockets I hastily put this landscape together and lock it inside my eyes. The gentleman and the lady must already have met. They are inside me, on a beach, walking hand in hand in the clear landscape. But on bringing into myself the distant shape of the mountains and the sea, I have also dragged in the avenue, the trees, the houses. Opening my eyes again and looking through the window I see that everything has disappeared. It's dark now. I have drawn into me the daylight too. I leave all that to wander around in my memory. I don't need to intervene in the fate of the young woman and the gentleman. Oblivion, like a sparrowhawk, is drawing circles around them. I leave the window. And I remember that during the day which has just ended I had been wandering around in search of a restaurant. I go back down into the street. Darkness has made people even more fluid. Men and women are as transparent as a dragonfly's wings. Thus is everything fragile. A gesture, an inconsiderate word, and the being who was standing in front of you is but a small puddle on the paving. We are constantly in the process of passing through someone or something. We are not only permeable. We are carried along too. If we left our mothers it was to enter another mother who carries us in her turn until another mother welcomes and encloses us. One after another, from one being to another and one thing to another (the mothers themselves are carried by other mothers, super mothers) we make our way towards a place that no one amongst us has yet imagined. And in passing through others we pass through ourselves. Then we're like a glove turned inside out, or like permeable earth which in a never-ending circuit is at the same time the earth passed through and the earth which passes through.

BODY AND SOUL

For Jean Tortel[1]

The body and the soul, dedicated to living together, do not always behave like friends towards one another. There are some inherent ills in the body. No one could question that there are other ills inherent in the soul. A certain part of the body hurts, for example. There are pains which strike the external, visible organs. Other pains arrive to bother our interior organs, invisible ones such as the liver, the spleen, the lungs. Obviously if you open up the body you can see these organs. But who can see his own organs? Whose eyesight, whose hearing are so powerful and so acute that he has been able to observe his own heart and hear—holding it in his hands—its beat? Of course, we have dissected corpses, we have seen animals which resemble us with internal organs like ours. But that proves nothing. Even if you open your own abdomen what could you see for certain through the fog of blood and bodily

1 Jean Tortel (1904-1993), French poet and essayist.

fluids? So it is easy to imagine that in addition to these organs there are others that are completely invisible: the soul's organs. For if the body's ills are different, the soul's ills are different too, depending on its part or organs under attack. Just as one can have a pain in the body's liver or heart or teeth, so too can one have a pain in the soul's liver or heart or teeth. The vagueness of the soul's suffering comes precisely from the impossibility of identifying which organs are suffering. And like someone who is convinced of the existence of his internal organs through the pain he sometimes feels, the certainty of the soul's existence is found in the vague suffering which can only come from it. Who amongst us has not heard someone (or perhaps oneself) say: I don't know what's wrong with me today, I'm overwhelmed with sadness for no reason; it's like a strange pain deep down inside me.

The close community in which the body and the soul exist means that the afflictions of one can be communicated to the other if they last for too long. Thus, the pains of the soul's organs sometimes attack the body's organs or vice versa. When there is a disagreement between the body and the soul the latter may rage against the former and choose a visible organ upon which to vent its wrath. The body can act against another body. It can give and receive blows. In the same way, the soul can act against another soul. It can attack it. It can also be attacked. But the soul can act not only against another soul but also against another body. In the same way that it can vent its anger on a visible or an invisible organ of the body it occupies, it can take vengeance for an offence on some other body. Certain people initiated into these mysteries through an oral tradition know how to make use of the soul's powers. Thus they can influence the sleep or the wakefulness of those around them. They can send dreams. There are the body's dreams and the soul's dreams. Sometimes an arm or a leg start to dream all by themselves. The liver dreams a liver's dreams. The lungs dream a lung's dreams. The sorcerers mix it all up. They give a heart's dreams to the lungs, a thigh's dreams to the heart. They give a man a tree's or a river's dreams. The man then feels in himself the quivering of thousands of leaves or the passing through him of shoals of small fish. Sparkling, he leaps over the stones. The soul too can dream that it's a body and as it's obliged by its high calling as a soul to behave in an exemplary way it can in its dreams as body finally give itself up to the worst debauchery and the worst follies. Thus the dreams of the body and those of the soul become entwined sometimes and on waking it is fairly difficult to disentangle the threads of one from those of the other. That is why sometimes one meets people whose gaze is vague and adrift: their eyes are those of their soul for their body's eyes have remained in their soul's face. But by the light of day when the man resumes his habitual activities the organs of his soul and his body gradually resume their proper places. Those are the japes which the soul likes to play sometimes, for it also likes to have a joke and make the person it inhabits unrecognisable to those around it.

"What's wrong with you this morning?" "I've no idea," is the response. Sometimes too his hair seems different, his face dissolves into the air, his gaze is like flowing water. It's his soul which is overflowing like a high tide, but at low tide his body finds its sand and earth again. Of course, it's difficult not to go against your own soul for you don't know where it is, you don't even know the shape and the extent of its organs. On the whole it's as if you were in a dark room, bumping into objects and furniture without realising it, for, unlike what is happening in the room, here it is the furniture and objects which suffer, and not you yourself. What have I done to that one? It's got something against me (and even if it's asked it can't itself tell you what it's got against you—it just knows it's something, that's all). It's that you've bumped against one of the organs of its soul. Then the soul throws out a cloud of ink, like an octopus, which casts a shadow over everything, making any contact impossible. You must only ever act whilst taking great precautions, for you never know where the soul may be. You never know what might damage the soul. But do you know what can damage the body? Not with any more certainty. A look, a smile can wound the body. That seems of no consequence. But then another person's smile can suddenly make you feel awkward, you slump, your posture becomes uncomfortable, you twist your hands and feet. There are people who have been turned into hunchbacks by a look. Others have been struck dumb by listening to someone laughing or crying. A woman fell ill because the man she loved had turned his head in a certain way on meeting her. We never know all the harm we can do without realising it. We never take enough precautions. We should constantly demonstrate politeness, sensitivity. The smallest thing can bring about someone's death. So never say, "I haven't done him any harm." But you have, you have trampled on his soul. The organs of the visible body take pity on the sufferings of the soul's invisible body. That is when blood drains from the face and from all the visible tissues in order to rush to the aid of the soul's invisible organs. The man becomes very pale, he staggers, he collapses. All his life force flows towards the soul. And only when the soul has recovered its calm, when the annoyance and hurt have been assuaged, does the blood make its way back and return to the body. One comes round then as if from a faint. But sometimes the harm done to the soul has been fatal and the body remains pale and unconscious for ever. The blood, yes the blood finds the secret door which leads it from the visible body to the soul's invisible body. Like a kindly being the blood feels for the soul and takes care of it. Taking the soul by the hand it guides it out onto the sunlit meadows, it makes it forget the hurts. That's why there is no longer any blood in the veins of a dead person. The adaptable blood with its multiple and fragile forms dresses the soul as if in a ball gown. Ah! Beloved woman, have I made you suffer! Have I struck your soul. You were pale and downcast, you were weeping and yet I'd done you no physical hurt. I'd simply said to you: I'm leaving you. And you threw me that long and pained look of a paralysed person whose heart is wrung to see the departure of the being whom he cannot follow.

MIRRORS

For Mickey Gros[1]

Don't trust mirrors. If you forget, if you try to escape, the mirrors remember, they stay in place. Women know that. They ask the men whom they love to embrace them in front of mirrors. That's one thing you must avoid doing. If you put your arms around a woman in front of the mirror you can never again disengage yourself. Everybody enjoys watching themself doing this or that in front of a mirror. The child makes faces. The young man wraps himself in romantic cloaks, makes eloquent gestures, plays the role he dreams of. The mature man looks at the stranger smiling pityingly at him, the white hair covering his forehead. The old man seeks in the cloudy waters of the mirror a man walking along a deserted path at the summit of which he expects to see a beloved figure appear. Each one of us is delighted to see themself from the outside, as if it were someone else. But the being in the mirror often replaces the real

1 The wife of Léon-Gabriel Gros (see footnote on page 56).

being. The mirror has magic powers and each one of us without realising it exposes themself to dangerous witchcraft. You calmly leave your house each morning after adjusting your hat and your tie in the mirror. Oh! Deceptive calm! You go off to your office or to your friends or about your usual business, with your untroubled conscience. And yet all this time the being in the mirror, who is you yourself, can indulge himself in the most unrestrained activities. Who knows if he isn't blocking the road to vehicles like a highway robber, or raping decent women, or setting fire to the houses of honest neighbours he takes to be enemies. But all that is nothing compared with the strength with which a woman attaches herself to you if you embrace her in front of a mirror. Those who run bordellos know this. It's why the rooms in these houses are lined with looking glasses. The woman's image is multiplied endlessly in the silver coating of these mirrors, and the man, who is also multiplied, has the triumphant impression that he's holding all the women in the world, the whole world, in his arms. He's surprised to see that it's he himself and the woman he holds in his arms, he even forgets that it's himself and is amazed to see himself increasing in size like a bird spreading its wings and covering the whole landscape with his passion. The woman becomes devilishly beautiful. Her body vibrates in front of the mirror like a violin. Her teeth bite the glass and the splashing of deep water is heard, disturbed by her legs and arms. The man disentangles himself from her embrace and leaves, dazed. But the one in the mirror continues his fun. So did I not hear once about a woman being impregnated by the reflection of a man in the mirror? He knew nothing about it, he went unconcernedly about his business, but during this time he was entangled in the woman's mouth like a drink and in her venomous eyes, against the backdrop of the mirror's fatal snows. That's why I advise those reading this text never to let themselves be taken in by the evil spells—so innocent in appearance—of a woman who likes to watch herself being embraced in front of the mirror. I have seen men who were faithful to their wives, fathers who were attached to their children, and who after embracing a woman in front of a mirror became unrecognisable. Nothing more than a ghost was circulating in the real world. The actual being had remained in the mirror attached by unbreakable ties to the body of a young sorceress. First, you have to avoid bordellos where there are many mirrors. Destroy those chambers where love and those who devote themselves to it are infinitely multiplied. But they deceive themselves who imagine you can put everything right by teaching husbands and lawful wives how to make use of the powerful magic of mirrors. It would be a clumsy solution to give your own house the appearance of a bordello with its arm-chairs and deep divans, its mirrors in which gestures go on for ever. If they did this, the husband and wife would become victims of their own witchcraft. Then everything would happen as if their house were no longer their house and as if two strangers had come to take their places. Sometimes during the evenings they would experience a vague embarrassment. Their children, with their greater sensibility, would show on their faces their distress at quickly realising there had been a substitution. Why are the mirrors covered up in the house of someone who has died? Is it not out of shame, for whilst the one who has departed this world is carried to his last resting place on a modest carriage drawn by a horse or an ox, his immortal double in the mirror is indulging in fun and games, illustrating his criminal indifference? The very design of the mirror allows all this mad behaviour for, whilst other natural objects appear with their shapes and sizes, all you see of a mirror is its surface. Who would think of mistrusting something as flimsy as a surface? No depth, no shape. A pointless illusion. It is the other things, that seem to have substance, which are nothing but a façade, fragile surfaces. Beneath its impassive and insubstantial reflection the mirror hides a universe of infinite depth and extent. It constantly brings you proof of the world's inaccessibility. Everything can happen in the same way whether in actual space or the reverse. For example, an object or a being increases in size on moving away and shrinks on approaching. The mirror turns everything round, clothes, furniture, bodies, souls. Nothing escapes it, no sign, no secret. The mirror recognises the traitor who stops in front of it to arrange his face confidently, smiling and saying to himself: no one will be able to read my evil designs in my look. If you hide stolen objects in your clothes you only have to stop in front of the mirror for them to be visible through the garments. My advice is addressed above all to those who are contemplating some risky course of action which could lead them to prison or to the scaffold. Burglars, dishonest cashiers who dip into their masters' coffers, corrupt servants who falsify their expenses, flirtatious women who deceive their men friends. They should all be careful around mirrors. For, unlike what happens to honest people who once they enter the mirror's open and limitless domain indulge in evil activities, dishonest people, perverts, liars, traitors, murderers, once caught in the mirrors' clutches become repentant, scrupulous people and prey to their own conscience. And when the thief thinks he's protected, his image in the mirror gives out signs, speaks and exposes his wicked ways to the justice of men. Thus if you enter a house with evil intentions, avoid the mirrors. Burglars who are forewarned already carry in their toolkit, along with their jemmy and bunch of keys, a mask to protect them from the revealing beams of mirrors. So never trust that appearance of a clear and shallow lake. Or else keep a close watch on your image, keeping on a leash like a dog. I'll never forget the day when in a moment of weakness I had allowed my image to sink into the mirror. I remained standing on the parquet floor in front of the large wardrobe in my parents' bedroom, afraid and ashamed. For the rascal which looked just like me had gone off into the far distance. Nothing held him back, not the linen in the wardrobe, nor the house walls, nor the ramparts of my childhood town. Do you think he was bothered about me waiting shamefacedly for him? Now and then, like a diver resurfacing with a knife or a shell between his teeth, he jumped up in front of my eyes, cocked a snook and plunged back into the sunlit landscape. Only the onset of night, which calms all anxieties, brought me solace in my sadness. Its merciful fingers effaced my features from the mirror, dragged back my image from its depths and attached it to my feet with delicate cords. Thus I was able to move away, dragging myself like a shadow, and I escaped from the mirror's magic power.

Perhaps all mirrors should be destroyed, or at least forbidden or their use limited. For mirrors have no respect at all for our laws and most honourable customs. An eminent luminary, festooned and splendid in all his life's and his era's glory, suddenly looks ridiculous and absurd in the mirror. The most beautiful woman suddenly sees in it someone looking like her covered in wrinkles and wearing rags. The pupil recognises in it the weakness and vanity of his teacher. The workman, the timid employee if they catch sight in it of their master's face suddenly understand how small and vulnerable he is. The convict observes in it the vacuity of his judges and his guards. Using a mirror endangers the most solid foundations of our lives. No magistrate, no wise man, no highly placed counsellor can escape it. What could be more disrespectful than that being who looks like the minister looking at himself in the mirror and doing cabrioles like a clown. On the other hand it is certain that attacking mirrors is not an easy thing. If you destroy the pewter which covers the glass, if you break even metal mirrors, if you disturb all waters so that their surface does not turn into the magical expanse, mirrors will still find a way to infiltrate themselves amongst us, in our streets, in our houses. No doubt there are mirrors which float in the air like great invisible birds.

From time to time they find a place or a thing which suits them and they make their nests there and become visible. Sometimes it's a black shiny piece of furniture where the mirror takes up residence. Sometimes it's a window into which the red evening light whips a flock of mirrors. Sometimes it's a drop of dew on a leaf where the perfidious mirrors ensconce themselves. Sometimes it's the shining skin of a cherry. Or else above a tomb, a piece of marble in which the sky and life move about and invent a thousand games with no regard for the suffering caused to the dead person. The battle with mirrors being so unequal, all that's left for us is to keep a close eye on them. Or if not, we shall have to change ourselves, have nothing more to hide, avoid these dualities, these multiple lives that inhabit us. Become genuinely honest and simple, with no obscene thoughts, no unthinking and forbidden desires, no treachery, no lies, so that the mirrors no longer have anything detrimental to discover in us and punish. Our elders, our teachers, our masters also have just to mend their ways in order to no longer be the easy prey of mirrors. Their vanity, their pride must give way to simplicity so that mirrors can no longer mock and expose to ridicule and even destruction our most respectable figures and principles.

TWO PERFORMANCES

For Antoine Goléa[1]

How many times have I not felt able to speak true words, to tear away the veil covering every aspect of the universe, understand others and understand myself! It was if a dizzy spell was taking hold of me, words spilled out of my mouth like an outpouring of blood, look, look in a moment I shall see what is not visible, name what has as yet no name. Then suddenly my vision was blurring, everything was frosting over, the world was getting away from me, disappearing into the distance. I was trying to work things out:

How have I behaved, what have I done or said which shattered the fragile links? I was the shipwrecked mariner who sees passing by his wreck the vessel which his cries fail to stop. Where does the fault come from? From me, no doubt, who went about it the wrong way. I tried to approach things on tiptoe; to look at them as if I wasn't there.

1 Antoine Goléa (1906-1980): A French musicologist of Romanian origin (real name Siegfried Goldman).

Perhaps it was my gaze which frightened them. So I watched them with my eyes closed. Perhaps it's also my hearing which frightens them. So I listened to them with my ears blocked. Thus I gradually gave up my sense of taste, of smell, of touch. Deaf, unfeeling, blind, had I also become invisible?

When watching a performance—at the cinema, in the theatre—I liked to concentrate not on the stars in the foreground but on those behind, the unknown bit players, the inexperienced beginners who are neglected and not yet discovered by the public. Sometimes I discovered some wonderful characters, faces expressing the soul's most elevated sentiments. Those with the starring roles, knowing themselves to be scrutinised by the audience, would take on studied attitudes, making gestures aimed at the admiring crowd.

But in the background, quietly and modestly, the bit players thinking their own thoughts, wrapped up in their own desires, their own miseries, would reveal a more animated, and more real world. Then I would dream of writing a play just for the bit players: whilst at the front two leading players would deliver a dialogue to elicit applause, behind, in the dimness, the bit players would perform another play, the real one, which the audience would hear and see on the quiet. Thus two plots would take place at the same time: the dazzling plot of the stars, the sole purpose of which is to attract attention and thus to deceive—and the secret plot of the bit players, revealed only to a few select people. There, there are heart-breaking passions and conflicts, there is life itself struggling and making its voice heard. And behind these bit players there are other characters who are to the bit players what they themselves had been to the stars, undiscovered characters and yet who are there and signal to us as if deaf and dumb.

Indeed, there are in the foreground of the stage of the universe itself shining in all their brilliance and glory famous artistes called mountains, trees, seas, rivers, forests, capital cities. So I learned to turn my gaze away from these starring roles and to concentrate on the bit players of the darkness, the silence and the solitude. I realised that from the highest point of the heavens down to the depths of the shadows the colourful and showy aspects of the universe are only there to deceive us and turn us away from another secret and distant universe which avoids our gaze and our breath.

It was a long and hard apprenticeship. For I had to try to blot out what I had been taught. Get out of the habit of seeing whatever forced itself upon my sight, of hearing what sounded in my ears. Not the trees, nor the stones, nor the flames, nor the water.

Here, behind this mountain and hidden by it, is another mountain, more splendid and more vast than the world. Inside this ocean, but greater than it, there is another ocean. Henceforth the thing to do was not to let myself be taken in any longer. Would I have the strength to resist the temptation? For the flowers were decked out in their most beautiful colours, the birds were singing, the trees were laden with fruit, the towns shimmered with all their towers and their cupolas. The sounds of rejoicing outside often came even into the poor man's hut. Who would not have been deceived?

Who would not have followed the glorious parade? And even those who shut themselves inside dark rooms well away from the celebrations, did they not harbour the secret hope, which they did not dare to admit even to themselves, that they would one day be acclaimed in the place of honour?

So there is something which despises our senses and does not yield to them. And that's when I understood the danger of language. Naming solely what is visible, audible, touchable, it becomes unsuitable for expressing what is invisible, inaudible, untouchable. As beneath each deceptive aspect there is another aspect, the real one, so beneath each word there must be another word, this time a secret one, which expresses the forbidden world.

I left the human race behind. I gradually took on the colour of the things surrounding me, I merged with the earth, with the rain, with the wind. Instead of the pleasure of hearing or making myself heard, I preferred that of being a pool of water, a heap of sand, a splinter of rock.

THE YOUNG EAGLE AND THE OCEAN PRINCESS

For René Massat[1]

One summer evening an old mother eagle was watching her latest son playing happily on the rocks. She was thinking of all her sons who were now streaking in glorious circles around the skies. They were far away now, attacking life as if it were a tough old panther. Powerful but sad, they reigned over desert regions. There were no affectionate looks to welcome them back from their long expeditions. There was no one to bind their wounds after their fierce fights. The old mother's heart bled when she thought of all that. She would have liked to bring her far-distant sons plenty of prey and to call to them with her eagle's cry: "Be happy! Live in peace."

Her sole remaining son had not yet tried his wings. He stood unsteadily on his flimsy feet. His talons were scarcely detectable and his body seemed too heavy for

1 René Massat (dates unknown), French writer and publisher. (Not to be confused with the French socialist politician 1934-2020.)

him. Now he circled his mother making small stammering sounds. "No, you're not going to fly yet," she was telling him. "You're too young. You need a lot of strength to fly. Wait until your wings grow, until they are like a large terrace you can stand on without trembling. Only then will you be able to overcome your light headedness and confidently face up to danger." The old mother knew there were a thousand dangers lying in wait for those who fly. The air is full of visible and invisible enemies. With every flap of their wings they could fall into the grip of a merciless attacker. She knew too that the further one is away from the earth, the more one risks coming face to face with massive killers. Far away, at great heights, there are huge beings hovering who seem to be obeying the orders of an inexorable law. The most courageous of her brothers and her sons had perished venturing there. One day she herself, forgetting her habitual caution, had flown beyond her normal limits. She had been flying over a lake. Perhaps it was a sea, for its banks were not visible. Looking down she could see through the clear water the dizzying marine depths. Her gaze revealed monsters moving to right and left and tearing apart innocent victims. And suddenly she realised that this lake was simply a mirror reflecting the enormous heights whose threshold she had just crossed. Yes, raptors with fluid wings were hovering over the azure waters and what she could see at the bottom of the lake was nothing more than the mirror image of these monsters.

High up, the earth and its charms no longer have any effect. No protest makes its way across these layers of space. Too icy cold? Too scorching hot? No one knows. And the old mother was thinking: every being—whether with wings or not—wants to rise above and clear the pull of the earth. The seed uses its tiny fists to strike the clay, it gasps, it pants, it begins to open out, small strands appear, the roots. And then the stem—apparently without effort—but at the price of what an extraordinary expenditure of strength—begins to grow. Higher, ever higher. And man, who as soon as his legs will take his weight stands upright and tries to touch the heavens with his forehead. They, and all the other beings who are tied to the earth, creeping along the ground or rustling leaves and branches, spend their lives wanting to take to the skies. Since they never succeed they cannot appear implacable. Their powerlessness is hidden beneath their hypocritical affability.

Small birds and those who live close to them in farmyards finally adopt the same habits. Thus they become sleepy, they gradually accept all sorts of cowardly ways and finally they even forget their impulse to fly. Then they stop growing. Objects and beings stay the same size. They even begin to shrink, to stoop towards the earth and in the end to return there.

Only we others, beings who fly towards the high frontiers, can not allow ourselves to be distracted from our labours. When earthly progress is done, flight, with its foaming wake through the skies, becomes for us another progress. But we are forbidden any light-hearted joy, any oblivion. We take on these dangerous exercises without any safety net. The slightest inattention means death. No time for wheedling, for courteous exchanges.

And the mother eagle remembered the large number of those like her who, having crossed into the forbidden zone, had not been heard from again. So lost for ever: dead? Perhaps. But what is strange is that their bodies were never found either.

She had arrived at this point in her musings when, glancing towards the spot where her son was, she gave a cry of horror. He had in fact left the rock, but instead of walking he had spread his quivering wings and was hovering in the air. The mother rushed frantically towards her son and, picking him up in her powerful beak, carried him back towards the rock. Her look was enough to convey her admonition and the youngster, embarrassed and ashamed, flapped his wings as if to say he was sorry. Overcoming her anger, the mother very carefully led the young son to her nest. There, she curled up next to him and in the hesitant and unadorned language of those who live alone she expressed her fears and her love. No, my little one, she said, don't fly yet. Wait a while. I'll look after you. I'll fly in your place. I'll always find food for you. To send him off to sleep she told him the story of the Sea Princess: Deep in the ocean, she said, in the palace of the king of all the seas, a beautiful princess was dying of boredom. The king, her father, had brought her the most splendid jewels. If at night the heavens sparkle with thousands of stars, these stars are nothing but the reflection of the incomparable gemstones surrounding the Ocean Princess in her palace . . . But the radiance of all these gemstones is quite dull in comparison with that of her eyes. And no pearl can compare with those nestling in the oyster shell of her mouth. Nevertheless all those in the palace were unhappy. For one day the Princess had gone for a walk around her kingdom and after rising to the water's surface she had gone to stretch out on the sand. Very high mountains towered into the air nearby. A young eagle who was lost also had also come for a walk along the Ocean edge. With his noble and proud bearing he looked like a prince. He came up to the Princess, bowed and asked her kindly what the place they were in was called. The Princess looked up at him and was struck by his dazzling beauty. The young eagle was no less struck by the Princess's beauty. After a few moments of speechless enchantment: "Follow me to the home of my father, the King of the Oceans," said the Princess. And she named the vast expanses of his empire. The eagle fell to the ground sighing with sobs of joy, caressing with his wings the princess's long train. He did not for a moment hesitate to accept the amorous invitation. Clinging to one another they were preparing to plunge into the water when a storm erupted. Lighting covered the sky and darkness suddenly descended, in place of the bright sunny day. You would have thought that thunder was shouting the orders. Shrugging off the embrace of his beloved, as if moved by an unknown force, the eagle took to the air. The storm stopped abruptly. It had lasted only for the few seconds when the eagle had touched the water. The Princess watched him flying higher and higher, making large circles and gradually becoming smaller until he was no more than a dot. But just as he was about to almost totally disappear the Princess saw a strange thing that filled her with fear. Far away at a great height the eagle began to grow bigger; from the dot that he had been he reverted to his normal size as if the distance no longer had any effect on him. He even outgrew these dimensions, becoming more and more enormous, totally covering the landscape and the skies. The horizon took on the shape of his wings and the sun became no more than a pale reflection in the blinding light of his plumage. Distraught at this sight, the Princess fell back into the waves and hurried back to her father's dwelling. From then onwards her torpor was like a slow death. The astrologers had looked into it and explained to the Princess that the young eagle could not come back to her by the same route as she had taken. That given the perfect arrangement of the other worlds, high up, beyond the permitted zones, there was the continuation of the ocean where she lived. So all the young eagle had done was to obey the voice of the thunder ordering him to cross the high-up oceans in order to arrive in the depths of the earthly ones. But the astrologers did not hide from the young princess the fact that terrible dangers were lying in wait for the one she had fallen for. And whilst reassuring her about the love the young eagle had for her, they refrained from asserting that her crazy enterprise would succeed. Nevertheless, all the courtiers, the ladies in waiting, the younger princesses, started work on the Princess's trousseau, whilst they awaited her fiancé, the young eagle. Lacework, brocades, delicate tissues, handkerchiefs lighter than cobwebs accumulated. To such an extent that the great gusts of wind that sometimes pass in the depths carried some of them away and raised them to the surface. It is since that time that those beautiful pieces of lace—called foam—appear on the crests of waves. All the underwater world continued to work on the Princess's trousseau but there was never any news of the young eagle.

And to finish her story, the mother added: "You see, son, if the young eagle had been content to see the beautiful Princess from time to time at the water's edge, he could still be happy. But he dared to take on the pitiless altitudes. He went where flight becomes so vast that it destroys the one who flies."

The young eagle, who had listened wide-eyed to this story, was quivering all over.

"So, mother," he said after a long silence, "if the ocean high up there is the same as the one below, won't the eagle find the Princess in the end?"

"What are you saying?" cried the mother, and to herself she was thinking, "Oh my God, was I wrong to tell him that story? I, who wanted to scare him—the young eagle crossed the frontier of the incurable monsters, the spirits and angels of annihilation. He'll find not the Princess but his own punishment."

In the days that followed the young eagle did not leave his rock. When his mother went hunting he would wait for her patiently. The mother eagle felt more and more reassured. Days and weeks went by without the young one trying to fly. Autumn was well advanced and the trees and the mountain tops were lit up with the silvery colours of the October festivals. November arrived with its rainy traps into which the fogs and mists dissolved silently, and blindly like great fish. The mother eagle went out less often and her heart sang with joy to see her son's faithful attachment to the earth. Thoughtful and serious, he kept constantly close to her, not spreading his wings, nor making any worrying gestures. And then winter arrived. No snow had yet fallen on the earth. But the wind blew with its sharp words like shards of glass and the pine trees leant to left and right like despairing monks.

And one day it began to snow. The mother eagle and her son, huddled together, were watching wordlessly as the first flakes fell. Everything was quickly covered in whiteness. But then what happened? At the same moment the young eagle and his mother recognised in the snow, covering with its whiteness the sky and the space beyond, the Princess of the Oceans who, wearing her dazzling trousseau, was going to meet her fiancé. They saw her clearly with her splendid lacework in which the foam of the waves was mixed with the delicate flowers of ice. Is it not the same water genius which is expressed in the ocean flutes and the snow trumpets?

Princess of the Seas, Princess of the Snows
You whose spume unites the earth and the heavens
The swans have followed your immaculate caravan
With your lips so cold and your eyes so fiery

We know that you're there just by this great silence
Which covers all things. And the blind man takes your hand
And recognises his future hope
On this keyboard with its keys of salt and wine

Princess of Love without pity and without hatred
Your bite is sweet to the man who follows you
You know no mercy and upon your long train
Your victims sing a hymn to the night

You appear so adorned and so noble at the windows
What more would be needed to madden us further?
The pine trees welcome you, the beech trees honour you
And the wolves fall fascinated upon your footprints

You still have the water's attributes: so transparent,
You are at once the thing seen and the being who wants
[to see
No mirror knows the gentle slope of your spirit
You who spread a glorious mirror in the air

You simply make the December hours pass by
Did you not precede the universe?
In your mouth the cold scent of mint and camphor
Those distant gratings shaken by the seas

Wherever you came from, the heights or the dark depths,
A high statue or one stranded by the tide on winter's prow,
For you, with his wings above the clear mountain tops
The eagle will trace his flight, a flight more secret than
[these lines.

What happened next was beyond the strength of the poor mother. With slow movements, without haste, her son had unfolded his wings. During the weeks which had passed since he had given up trying to fly, his wings had grown. He was so handsome and so graceful that his mother could not help letting out a cry of admiration. But he was no longer looking at her. He went to the edge of the precipice below his rock and began to glide. He traced a large circle inside which he seemed to lock the snow which was still falling. He made this circle several times, as if inspired by some magical science. And, in fact, outside this circle the snow stopped. The snow, the white-foamed female statue, were no more than a column which the young eagle's flight surrounded as if inside a ring. Snow and eagle were now burning with a single flame. Then the bird began to soar, and the mother saw with fear how to start with he became smaller, only to then swell immeasurably until he covered the whole landscape. The horizon had become an immense white bird and it was no longer possible to see whether it was the Princess of the Ocean and the snow, or the young eagle, or the two together who were rising as one into the eternal whiteness.

WHY SHADOWS ARE BLACK

For Jean Mazenq[1]

One evening Yves was sitting in front of his bedroom door looking at the sky. A star-studded horizon had taken the place of the day's summer sunshine. Close by the birds were practising their song. Nothing came to disturb the harmony of the celestial songs responding to the music which trembled like fire in the throats of the winged musicians.

Soon, amidst this nocturnal jubilation, Yves almost had the impression that he had crossed the space which separated him from the heavens. Around him he felt a vague intangibility and was amazed to see that the stars were not, as he had previously thought, solid objects, but phosphorescent clouds, hazy accretions amongst which he was moving with a sense of calm and happiness. It was in this state that his friend, the shepherd Edouard, found him—"I'm star bathing,"

1 Jean Mazenq, Humanist teacher, writer and artist. Town clerk of Moyrazès, close to Rodez in the Aveyron, 1941-1964.

said Yves to him. "It's so good to hide in this celestial lucerne."

"Each one of us is a star, and each star is a human being," the shepherd replied gravely. "Yes, men stars are below, and star men are above. Invisible threads link them to one another. Each movement of a man on the earth corresponds to a movement of a star in the sky. When you hear someone say, 'I don't know what's wrong with me today, I'm sad for no reason' it's because he can feel inside himself the unknown sadness of a star. We are affected by the stars of our friends and by those of our enemies. When the enemies on earth seem to be keeping quiet their stars—second-guessing their intentions, influence us for good or ill. They know acids—apparently harmless ones—which corrode stones, bones, metals. But at the same time, the stars suffer from our own rivalries and our hatreds."

"I take from what you say," Yves exclaimed sadly, "that neither the stars nor men can heal the wounds in our souls. And yet! The sky is so beautiful in this immutable night. I make a sign to my brother from on high. I send him the light which is quivering inside me and he sends me his."

I'll tell you a story about these lights. To start I must remind you (and I learned what follows as much from the book of the heavens as from the books of men) that each celestial or earthly body radiates light. Whether this is its own light, or one it receives from a more luminous body, from a burning sun and which it in its turn spreads around itself, this light when in contact with another body forms a shadow. Every day you see your shadow thrown by the sun. You have also seen your shadow thrown by the moon's beams (which according to astronomers does not have its own light but that reflected from the sun). A practised eye can see on a moonless night a shadow thrown by starlight. That shadow is scarcely discernible, but if it is less intense it is no less real. Imagine a really weak light: the shadow which arises from its contact with an opaque body will also be very weak. A light which is imperceptible to the eye: the shadow will also be imperceptible to the eye. My body for example emits light but your eye doesn't see it, neither does it see the shadow of your body thrown by the light from mine.

I can tell you too that each light gives off a different shadow (not in terms of intensity—everyone knows that—but in terms of its substance, the very quality of the shadow). We don't have, as is generally believed, a single shadow but an infinite number of them: the shadow thrown by the light of the sun, that thrown by the light of water, that thrown by the light of a tree, that thrown by the light of a stone, that thrown by the light of a scent. The shadow thrown by a young woman, the shadow thrown by a peach, the shadow thrown by a snake, the shadow thrown by fire and that thrown by snow, in short, as many shadows as there are objects, beings or phenomena around us. We know only the sad and dreary shadow which follows us in its mourning attire. But it was not ever thus. Previously men would walk along surrounded by their magnificent shadows like feathers round the head of an Indian warlord. They were handsome with their red, green, purple shadows, with their velvet shadows, with their greengage shadows, with their aroma-based shadows.

In days long gone by there was a young prince who had succeeded in gathering together some of the most beautiful shadows of his kingdom. For there existed then a scientific method, lost to us nowadays, for extracting the shadow like the sap from a plant or like the sound from a violin. Sometimes the prince would dress in the shadow given by a diamond's radiance: it was a shadow in which flames and water mingled their glittering sheaves. At other times he would put around his shoulders the shadow thrown by a dove's flight: that was a shadow in which the snow and the azure of the skies entwined their colours. The prince stored all his precious shadows in a closet and kept the key with him at all times. One day, however, when he had to go away for a distant hunt, he gave the key into the safekeeping of one of his pages, asking him to open the closet from time to time so that the shadows could benefit from the sun's beneficial light. He himself took on this journey only the black monastic shadow, as much out of fear of spoiling the sumptuous and flamboyant shadows as of frightening the game.

The day after his master left, the page, whether out of curiosity or out of a wish to do his duty, opened the doors of the closet. What he then saw was a delight to his eyes. Shadows like dazzling clothes. Silks, golds, the most beautiful velvets in the world. Here were shimmering diamond spangles, there rubies and topazes conjured up summery gardens, here the sunset radiated its soft fabrics, there dawn beat its drums. Here autumn's sombre tones were sounding, there spring was tuning its lutes. The page stood for a long time gazing at these riches. He dreamed of them all day long. In the evening, as he was going to meet his fiancée, he had an urge to be seen in finery worthy of his love. "Master won't know anything about it," he said to himself. "I'll take one shadow for myself and one for my true love, and before dawn I'll put them back where they belong." And indeed, he put on a red shadow the colour of a twilit summer evening, threw over his arm a white shadow with gold tassels for his fiancée and went to meet her. The young woman was just as bowled over as the young page. That evening their lovemaking was more intense than previously. It was as if, dressed in the prince's shadows, they felt themselves becoming more noble and more beautiful beings. But just as they were setting off on the way home, a strong wind suddenly got up. They were crossing a field with tall grasses. The beautiful shadows were not very tightly tied on, the wind lifted them off and the fearful young people realised that they couldn't find them. "Let's go home," the young page said finally, "I'll come back to look for them tomorrow morning." Early the next day the page went back to the place where the two shadows had been dropped. He found them, in fact, but that did him no good. The shadow he had been wearing had been transformed into a field of red poppies, the one worn by his fiancée had become a field of narcissi. It is since that time that poppies and narcissi have existed. The beauty of those fields in which the red of the poppies was singing in harmony with the azure-white of the narcissi was no consolation to the poor page. He was in despair all day. But in the evening, when he was due to meet his fiancée, his anxiety subsided. "The prince has so many other magnificent shadows that he won't even notice the disappearance of those two." And he went to the closet to borrow two other shadows, intending of course to return them when he came back from his walk. This time he took a pale blue shadow for himself and a dark blue one for the young woman. How happy it made her! She seemed more beautiful in the intangible fabric. She who had only modest shadows (I must add that alongside our dull ones even those were incomparable) now saw herself with a truly princely shadow. The two young people climbed into a boat. But this time once again the wind got up. The shadows fell into the water and the page tried in vain to fish them out. The next day he found in their place lotus leaves and water lilies. He was in despair, but the despair calmed down by the evening. "Master has so many other shadows," he said to himself, "he won't suspect anything." And every evening for a whole week he borrowed two of the prince's most beautiful shadows which he never managed to bring back to the closet. Sometimes these shadows became lilies, sometimes they became roses, sometimes they were transformed into rhododendrons, sometimes they even became clouds.

When the prince returned from his distant hunting ground: "Is all in order in the closet?" he asked the young page. But the page fell at the feet of his master, unable to lie. Speechless, he had only his tear-filled gaze to beg forgiveness. The prince opened the closet and saw that the most beautiful of his shadow finery had disappeared. "Tell me the truth," ordered the prince in a fury. And the page told him how he had been fascinated by the beauty of the shadows and how he had borrowed some of them for himself and his fiancée and how these shadows had become poppies, narcissi, water lilies, roses, clouds. The prince went to the fields and looked at the flowers. He looked up to the sky and recognised one of his shadows which had become a beautiful unmoving cloud. "I forgive you," said the prince, "for I'm delighted by the terrestrial flower clouds and the celestial cloud flowers. But you will nevertheless be punished. You and all my subjects, your fellow men, from now on will have only black and charmless shadows. I will get myself more shadow finery, but so that such a misadventure does not recur I shall make them invisible. These beautiful shadows will continue to exist, they will surround us with their flames and their colours, but no one will see them." And as the prince was something of a magician, he did as he had said.

That is why, since that time, even if one of us wears a wonderful shadow thrown by the brilliance of a diamond or by the sea's reflection, we are nevertheless seen to drag behind us only that sad black shadow—mute, deaf and blind.

COLOURS

For Thérèse Aubray[1]

The townspeople did not sleep well. The sky was covered with soot and near the cemetery, in the grass, miserable goats were grazing. There was never any sunshine and all was grey and dirty in the streets. The town was dark with dismal houses and shops. Early in the morning a crowd would enter the smoke-filled factories, and leave in the evening, haggard and weary. Upon their arrival in this world, children were dressed in dark-coloured materials. Very soon their faces would become sallow, their eyes would lose their brightness. Even voices were dull and hoarse.

Once day a stranger on foot entered the town's gates. He went up and down the streets crying: "Colours! Who would like some colours?" He would stop from time to time, put a small flute to his lips, and sounds full of gaiety were produced. "Colours, who wants some colours?" The townspeople would gather around him

---

1 Thérèse Aubray (1888-1974), French writer, poet and translator

and watch in astonishment as he waved small multi-coloured flags. Red, blue, yellow, white, green leapt from the stranger's hands like so many flames and fountains. The townspeople's eyes, which had never before seen any other colours than the dismal grey of their streets, could not take in both objects and colours at the same time. The colours seemed to them to be separate, independent of the things they covered, they themselves becoming *things* or *beings*. The stranger stretched out his hands: "Look at this colour . . ." he said, showing an orange. A child took it, and after cutting it he bit into it. "This colour is delicious." Eyes were already opting out and other senses rushed to celebrate the colours. The women wanted to touch the fabrics the stranger was exhibiting and they learnt about soft colours, rough colours, warm colours, cold colours. There were velvet colours, silken colours, stone colours . . . "Do you want colours?" the stranger was saying. And he showed them pinks, lilacs, basilisk, dahlias, geraniums. So the colours gave off a scent and all were filled with wonder. "What do you think of this one?" And there were colours that growled like thunderstorms, others which whispered like leaves, others you could scarcely hear like tiptoeing footsteps in a garden. "Look at this one now . . ." And the stranger made an expansive gesture, like an illusionist, and blue waves appeared. They came up onto the sand and the spume spread, laughing, in a single breath. This colour is called the Ocean.

There was a whole language being woven around the colours. All those looking at the colours were like dumb people having speech restored to them. "Here is the colour of separation," the stranger was saying. "Here's meeting someone . . . Here's the one of regret . . . Here's the colour of memory, and colour of sleep . . ." Everything was becoming simple, understandable.

Great celebrations took place that day, and on the following days, in honour of the stranger. "Tell us about colours," the townspeople would say. And the stranger, standing on a platform in the main square, named the wind, and it was the brown colour of the pine tree tops, then he named the twilight, and it was the gentle lowing of the herd around the sheep pen. He named the snow, and the sleigh bells tinkled, and roads were fashioned out of champagne glasses.

What joy from that time on in the town . . . "Stay with us," people would say to the stranger. And the children, instead of going to school, would come to him to learn to play the harp of colours. The women were becoming more beautiful, and their lips were now red. "Farewell, farewell" the stranger said to them, "I must visit some other gloomy towns." And he made birds of innumerable colours fly around his head. And, like a lamplighter who, after lighting up a whole district, goes off towards other streets, the stranger, after distributing colours to the women and children and even to the stern men, wrapped himself in his brilliant raiment of colours and set off towards another town . . .

INITIATION INTO DEATH

For Gaston Ferdière[1]

I am not going to talk about death, but about the moment which just precedes it. For neither day, nor night, nor the burning sun, nor the cloud-filled night can adorn us with a more sumptuous raiment. It is the moment when the tree consumed by flames hesitates between its noble form and the vague shape of ash. Then, all its fibres stretch out with extraordinary intensity. Its knots unfurl, its ligatures crack and its whole being opens up in an infinite radiance of life, rears up, leaves behind its own outline as if to attain the limitless and immutable form of its own perfection. All around it the flames come and go, busying themselves wordlessly, stopping, twisting, their gestures pleading and weary with separation. Or with those encouraging retreat as if to say: "It's this way, follow me." Already, almost all its strands are broken. Which roots, however strong they

1 Gaston Ferdière (1907-1990). French poet and doctor, close to the surrealist movement, who worked at the psychiatric hospital in Rodez.

might be, could prevent the tree from flying away when its branches are being transformed into wings of fire? For a whole burning forest becomes a giant bird taking flight. It circles for a few moments in the air before disappearing beneath a horizon of ash.

Oh! Objects, and you, men, how that flaming forest resembles you. Is it not the living fire of death which leads you towards eternal unity? Who has not felt, coming close to a dying man, a fire's heat?

The fire in this case is invisible but the dying man has almost left the room. He gets out of bed, he passes through the group of relatives and friends around him, who do not doubt that the person lying before them, even if he's still moving and talking, has no longer anything in common with the one who is leaving. He stops at the threshold. He glances indifferently, mixed a little too with surprise, at visitors and objects. He shrugs his shoulders as he sees himself struggling on the bed amongst the tangled threads of his life. He is already in the antechamber, he opens the door to the road. Here, he is slightly gripped by fear. Everything appears as if through smoked glass. Vehicles, men walking at an even pace like objects falling into a vacuum. Is it vertigo making him hesitate? The town seems light-headed, like him. It is only just making contact with the earth. Uncertain, he stops at the top of the street. Should he go right or left? Here is the square with the town's theatre, all lit up and the crowd surging around its entrance. He worms his way amongst the people waiting in silence with their serious faces and leaden bodies. "Come on, smile," he murmurs and his breath stirs the women's dresses. From here the town spreads in all directions like a fruit bursting out of its skin. The boulevards lead to the riverbanks. To the south a tree-lined avenue runs alongside the prison's high walls. All that can be seen are a few barred windows and the silence that reigns there is like that of a graveyard. The townsfolk keep well away from this district, which is gradually becoming detached from the town, forming a separate world with its own calendar and seasons. The dying man senses beyond the walls a huge white and still courtyard. He wants to see it. He pulls himself up onto the walls and now he's inside, moving amongst the guards who have no inkling of his presence.

A prisoner is sitting despondently on a stone, with his head in his hands. "Won't you come and play with me?" the dying man calls to him. And he climbs up the walls several times to show him that it's easy to get away. "Don't be scared. The watchmen won't be able to do anything about it. I too was stuck in bed and nobody stopped me leaving. Soon you'll be like me." The prisoner, deep in his bitterness, doesn't hear a word of this. The dying man skips around a guard a bit more, snatches off his cap ("Bloody wind!" the guard exclaims); and, laughing, he jumps over the wall on goes off again to stroll around the town.

Now the town is a huge leaf being nibbled by its hungry streets like caterpillars. He slips into the windows of the department stores, he bathes in the tepid rivers of silks, plays with the thousand toys he used to love so much without being able to go near them. At one moment he decides to choose as his home the window display of a furniture store. The passers-by glance in distractedly. He is sure none of them can see him. The shiny table, set with porcelain and crystal, invites him to a feast without end. There is an oak dresser, its doors closing upon mountains and cascades. Behind it there is a mirrored wardrobe. Careful! This one is dangerous! And indeed, turning his head sharply, the dying man sees in the mirror his face from before. If he is already invisible to the eyes of men, he is not yet invisible to the mirror's eyes. He has changed a lot: he's almost unrecognisable: his cheeks are sunken, his forehead transparent and showing the blood vessels like the last filaments of a spider's web spun in a hurry. He looks out into the street to see if anyone has noticed this image in the mirror reflecting nothing obvious. "I left too soon," he says to himself. And, regretfully, he leaves the shop window and makes his way towards his home which is already very dark and falling into ruin. He slides in amongst the visitors and stretches out on the bed like a shroud, upon his own corpse.

NO STAYING AWAKE!

For Lucien Becker[1]

Previously, as I was dropping off to sleep, a large bird would sneak into my bedroom. It was no good bolting doors and windows shut. It was no good staying wide awake in the shadows until the darkness pierced by my gaze was hanging raggedly and spattering my face and hands with its black blood. The bird would catch my slightest moment of inattention, taking advantage of it to burst into my bedroom and throw itself onto my bed, covering me with its ash black wings. Ah! Jerking awake on hearing a vehicle accelerating away, on recognising at the window the torn curtain of this velvety flight. How often did I awaken, wide-eyed, watching the thick smoke of darkness dragging itself like a big cat, its belly heavy with its earthly sins. Outside, the bird would be circling like a storm. Did it perch on the roof? The beams were creaking, the wind and rain rattling the windowpanes.

1 Lucien Becker (1911-1984), French poet and friend of Voronca.

I finally worked out how it went about passing through the closed doors and the windows: it came up to them, waited motionless for a few moments, then began to dissolve into the air. It was rather like a stain spreading over the black fabric of the night, but blacker than that fabric. As it was dissolving outside, so it was being reconstituted inside. Like an echo, not of sound but of matter. Here it is losing a wing, a claw, its beak. Then in the bedroom wing, claw and beak are reassembling. Thus by a strange osmosis the bird would finally enter the bedroom. Sometimes the cat's miaowing would scare it and it would abandon its transformation. Then part of the bird would remain outside, another part, more alarmingly than usual, would be close to my bed. The bird, having only one wing and one claw and only half of its horrible head, was twice as brutal and greedy as the whole bird. Daybreak would take the two parts of the bird by surprise, and they would rush to join together again and the violent sound of their reuniting would be heard in the dawn, wounding the firmament and covering it with blood.

As for me, with my lacerated body and face, bleeding, eyes rolling, I was getting up from the sheets. I no longer knew if it was day or night; if my life was coming to an end or just beginning. One night I shoved beneath my sheets a tailor's dummy the same size as me, I created my habitual disorder in my bedroom and, sure that any intruder would be taken in by my piece of trickery, I went out. Hiding in a bush I began to watch for the arrival of the bird. The bats were circling around me like black goblets, pouring out the viscous liquid of their contours. The air had become thick and heavy beneath the weight of darkness. I was trying hard not to sink into a tired sleep. I had fixed the point of a sword under my chin to stop my head drooping down onto my chest. And yet suddenly a large piece of darkness broke off and slapped me full in the face. Scattered feathers covered my clothes. A powerful breath dragged me from the ground and before I could think about or understand anything, I found I was back in my bed, tormented, lacerated by the deadly bird. But in the whirlwind which had carried us both through the walls the impetuous bird had lost its wings. Its body was smooth and its whiteness lit up the night. Its body was like that of an adolescent girl with firm curves, and the suffering it inflicted on me that night filled me with delight. Suddenly, I no longer felt oppressed, a great breath of liberty brought me back to life. In the light of dawn appearing at the windows the beautiful and lithe girl, humiliated and ashamed, wrapped herself in some old rags which straight away took on the copious outline of two wings. She floated effortlessly up to the ceiling which became a dawn sky, and disappeared. And I understood then the nature of my victory: I had tasted joy amongst my suffering. I was now wishing for darkness to fall so I could find again the magnificent young girl/bird. But she did not come again. For several nights in a row I waited for her. Whereas previously I had been making efforts to remain awake and to surprise and prevent the intrusion of the violent bird, now I was seeking at any price the sleep which would have favoured its arrival. But I could not get to sleep. So here I am, lying in bed, despairing, covered with the icy perspiration of sleeplessness. Night has no hold on me and on the things around me. The sun can fall into the deepest abyss, the trees can pass from branch to branch the dense networks of fog and mist, no shadow comes to calm the torment of my perception. The onset of night no longer works for me. The shapes of daylight are constantly before my eyes.

Ah! Sleep, when will you return, incomparable bird, to lacerate me with your claws, to plunge into my heart the dagger of your kiss. I did not know before that your flight, the beating of your wings, your hair with its mixture of stars and herbs would be such an intoxicating poison for me. If you have left my home forever, I shall come looking for you myself. If night and sleep refuse to come inside these walls, I shall go to other countries where night reigns eternally, where the nest of the bird-woman erects its wailing, laughing columns. I no longer fear your gloomy waters. I call to your curses, your crimes, your fires and floods like a shipwrecked mariner awaiting rescue or a pitiless wave atop the tallest mast of his ship. I'm waiting for you, large bird of my sleep, upon the high mast of my wakefulness. I drag myself along in the daylight's clarity as if in a foaming torrent. But at the end of it you are there, bountiful sea, limitless ocean of the night, you the magnificent woman-bird, you my death sentence and my blessing.

THE SECRET CITY

For Luc Decaunes[1]

We are exiles. Driven out of a far distant country whose climate, geographical location and even name we have gradually forgotten. Yes, we no longer really know the name of that country. Years and years have passed since the day we left. But now we are tormented with terrible nostalgia. Then we get together and each of us tries to dig a fragment of that country out of their memory. It's like a jigsaw puzzle where the pieces no longer fit together very well. The country where we are now wraps its reality around us, inviting us to look at and love it. But nothing attaches us to it. Objects and beings are before our eyes, but it's as if the power of our gaze were too strong for them. Like beams emanating from the same point which grow further and further apart, our gaze reassembles landscapes and people on a greater scale. In the distance we see the vast squares, the houses and the giant inhabitants of the lost city. Above the

1 Luc Decaunes (1913-2001), French poet and writer, a friend of the surrealists.

world where we continue to live we thus create another world towards which our thoughts are drawn. This created world is fragile and very often vague. The things, the clothes we brought with us into exile are worn out and we finished by dressing like the locals, picking up their habits, speaking their language. However, deep down we behave as if nothing has changed. It seems to us, when we get together, that we are still wearing the clothes and making the gestures of our far distant country. But what is that country? Some of us place it beside the sea. A sea unlike any other. With waves like an orchestra making music on the cliffs and on the beaches.

Many of us think that the unforgettable city is on a plain open to the seasons, but which the winds treat gently, like flocks of sheep suddenly recognising a magic sign and stopping in the middle of the countryside. The storms do in effect make great detours so as not to disturb this town's monuments. In one of the squares, in the middle of the built-up area, is a fountain, surrounded by dazzling streetlights; from here avenues branch off in all directions like beams of light from a star. And as those beams touch walls and forests in the darkness, waking them suddenly and making them visible, so the magic wands of these avenues bring to life the fine palaces and magnificent parks. Here happiness is like a stone rippling its circles in the water. It stretches further and further, going as far as the distant suburbs, to the edge of the town, to the working-class parts, breathing its liberty and peace. The city was built brick by brick by generations devoted to wisdom and fraternity. In its great halls musicians, painters, dancers get together. Hangings cast a calming glow onto the walls. The sun taps on the door like a young peasant man, entering the hallway with his shoulders bearing baskets of fruit and noisy birds. Nevertheless no one gets carried away. The crowds keep a dash of moderation and silence to their joyful masculinity. They reserve part of their happiness for those who have none. That is why the gaze of the townsfolk retains a noble gravity. The townsfolk know that aside from those who have never been to this town and who are unaware of its very existence, there are thousands of their brothers who have been banished from it. Over the course of its millennia the city has suffered the blows of numerous assailants. Envied for its supreme joyfulness, it was invaded by neighbours for whom it wished no more than that they should share its happiness and its wisdom. It had no other weapons or fortress than the brilliance of its arts and its music. The invaders began by wanting to lay waste to everything but were finally won over by the city's charm and magical qualities, even becoming its amiable citizens. The exiles, all alone, were no longer able to find their way home. And it was for those exiles that the happiest thoughts of the townsfolk were tinged with gravity and a little sadness.

Let each one of us try to remember. Let us form a circle
And let each one tell of happiness, of joy
Let us put our city back together like a lost book
Of whose pages each one can recite a short passage.

Now I'm listening to the description of a house
And I recognise the garden of my childhood
And the room where laughter spreads its brightness
And light like golden quinces on the dresser.

Perhaps it was the sound of harnesses at daybreak
Oh! The gentle neighing of horses being hitched
Waking is so sweet it's more like still dreaming
Seated in the freshness of summer's carriage.

At the crossroads gather the holiday crowds
Oh! The outing holds out its greenery to us
We make a halt near the stream, we break bread,
I swear it's my soul singing in the guitar's music.

Yes, let us remember that. Never forget the silence
And gravity of Autumn's park
And the hills decked out like brides
In the veils and crystalline robes of the grapes.

Evoke if you wish the tree-lined streets
With the acacia's perfume like a flight of doves,
With the birds tracing their ever-narrower evening circles
To make their nests.

Music pouring forth from the window, the sudden
Joy which takes you unawares in the twilight,
When the first lamps to be lit are hooks
To prevent the sky's linen from flying away.

When one has all the riches of the evening's length
When each smiling face is a haven
When one walks fearlessly along life's tightrope
For the friendship of men is weaving a safety net.

We have found once again the blissful town
Which we had lost, and like bees
Building the hive for their honey, the words
Of our mouths have constructed courtyards, avenues,
[gardens.

Like him who before making mortar and cement
Before laying the bricks sketched the births
And the galas and the gatherings of the future dwelling,
We evoke the joys of a still empty plot of land.

It's a town, a country, a continent, it's the globe
That our luminous homeland will cover
What does it matter if the places have been taken, we shall
[know that that joy
Will hoist it on the highest mast of the universe.

THE TWO OLD WOMEN

For G. Subervie[1]

The day was dying but the lamps were not yet lit. I got up from my work table and leant over the balustrade at the French window. In the street, where the last rays of the sun gave off a dim light, the crowds were walking slowly like a river's waters nearing its mouth. Soon they would pour into the ocean, giving themselves up to the night. There were young men coming home from work. Clerks carrying packages under their arms. Women coming out of shops after making their purchases. A few solitary figures dawdling, looking in shop windows. A group of schoolchildren ran past, pouring out the vowels of their laughter. Suddenly I saw two old women coming along from the top of the street. With their arms round each other's waists they were walking steadily, sliding along gently like ice skaters dancing. They were coming along the middle of the road and I could clearly see their long very white hair drawn into

1 Editor and publisher in Rodez.

two thick plaits on their heads like two royal crowns of snow. They were dressed in black. But their sombre clothing took nothing away from their joyful vivacious looks. For a transcendent glow, like a flame of eternal youthfulness, seemed to emanate from these two old women. I could not tear my gaze away from them. The crowd was becoming indistinct, retreating into the distance, disappearing even, so that all that remained to be seen was the image of those two old women walking along with their light and happy footsteps. They passed my window and approached the corner and were about to vanish when I noticed that their feet were not touching the paving. And as they were stooping so as to be closer to each other I recognised the humps made beneath their blouses by their folded wings. Then it was as if I was dazzled, blinded. A great silence reigned over all the street and I understood that in the crowd, talking and laughing gently, two angels had passed by.

NOTES

"When I like something I give myself up to it unreservedly," the sensualist was saying. "I give myself up to a book, I give myself up to a woman, and I give myself up to a landscape. And when at table I'm served a dish that I like I give myself up to it to such an extent that it's no longer me eating it, but the dish eating me."

That prosperous-looking man seated at table with his family would say, serving himself with the largest portions, "I must look after my children's father."

The similarity between a mirror and a serpent: if broken into pieces, both continue their vigorous life in each of the segments. And, like the mirror, does not the serpent bewitch the faces which are outside him and which, once reflected in its gaze, become its victims?

I had a rendezvous with my friend, L.P., who is lame. And at the time of our meeting I saw a lame person—who was not L.P.—walking towards me. It's L.P., I thought, sending me his lameness in advance to let me know he's coming. And indeed, a little time later, L.P. himself appeared.

Close up, this woman was young and beautiful. But if I moved two or three steps away from her, she aged by ten years. At a distance of twenty steps her face appeared totally wrinkly, her hair white and her body emaciated and bent. To stop this spell working I had to rush quickly towards her and hold her tightly in my arms to eliminate any space between us. Then she would glow again with freshness and charm. "Stay close to me," she would say to me without being aware of the destructive effect which distance had on her being.

And I would be plunged into great sadness.

A six o'clock in the evening the garden was peaceful, with the shadowy movement of children playing and the maids, the mothers and the layabouts idly gossiping. It wasn't really a garden, but rather a large square with just a few trees and surrounded by pieces of waste ground at the far end of which loomed the high buildings of the Stock Exchange and the Post Office. There were no benches but large iron armchairs, and the park attendant passed from one to another in her calm way with all sorts of talk and excuses and without insisting. People shook their heads and she went away. It was good to think that this was all happening as if I had not been there. No one was paying me any attention and I felt myself becoming invisible. And the square itself with its calming crowd was perhaps no more than an invention of my own gaze. Perhaps too I had got there too soon and this was all just a foreshadowing.

I was seeing this place and its crowds as they would be a hundred or two hundred years later. I took a few steps towards the street and, indeed, the square with its seats, its walkers and its children disappeared, leaving no trace. Will I ever know if this was a vision of the past, of the present, or of the future?

I thought I loved the piano. The piano was wave-like shoulders or sleepy serpents above a keyboard. And I listened to it and I watched it with passion: the piano. All the world's unhappy sighs seemed to vibrate on its strings. And as soon as the chords of a piano sounded in my ears from the window of some distant house in a crazy district the image of V. took hold of my being. How unreal was all that. I'd arrived at the point when I could not listen to any other instrument than the piano.

The flute seemed strained to me, fading away like a stem without sap. The ocarina would jump about somewhere in a dark room where only the eyes of a giant cat gleamed. The saxophone wept and laughed at the same time and became a negro in the grip of a sexual spasm, with chattering teeth. But the violin! It tried to call out to me, it sometimes sounded the first syllable of the precious name, it even threw out a familiar word, but I spurned it. It irritated me. Its resemblance to S.'s body was striking. If it had had arms it would have stretched them out towards me: was it not beneath the portent of the violin that I first encountered you, endearing and timid.

I speak your name, violin, and suddenly I find myself in a room looking over a dark courtyard: it's six o'clock in the evening, I've finished my schoolwork and from the windows opposite comes towards me, like a ray of light, the lament of a violin. I love these awkward notes, this ungainly hand I imagine trembling upon the bow. It's raining gently and the violin's stuttering mixes with the rain's pattering. It's a modest room, there's an adolescent with long hair and everything is bathed in a forest's October light. The violin! I saw it at a street corner in the hands of the long-suffering beggar. I saw it in the small modest restaurant, the humble violinist at the door allowing just the sound of the violin to enter, like a dog going ahead. "Would there be a little bit of bread?" Oh! Humane violin. Oh! Pretentious, overbearing piano. Inhumane piano. You are made for idlers, for the powerful, for the heartless. You require a great hall, you despise the furniture around you. And even in your old age when your teeth are falling out you cast your scornful and haughty look around you. No, it's not you that a beggar could drag with him amongst the murky crowd. You are indeed the image of that cruel woman, V. And in the orchestra, do you not always try to drown out the other sounds? But the violin! That's you, S., modest, delicate. It's you I should love. And I take you in my arms, I am the blind musician whose bow moves, distant and unearthly, like his gaze.

I don't know anything more clothed than a naked body. Rip the coat from a woman's shoulders, tear away her dress, remove the most intimate pieces of lace, and her body will shrink further and further away from you, it will finally close down like a lock the combination of which nobody knows. Perhaps the body is like those drawings which only appear when the sheet of paper is covered by another sheet of a certain colour which eliminates some shapes and makes others more visible. With what power do the breasts, the knees, the arms of a woman reveal themselves through her clothes? The fabric lends an incandescence to the body, the hair hisses like a black serpent, enchanting the white dove of her neck, making the crazy partridges of her elbows shiver, dragging itself insidiously as far as the soft firmness of her thighs. Taunting, audacious, sure of itself, shameless, tyrannical, talkative, open-minded—the clothed body. Veiled in shadow, taciturn, distracted, shut off—the naked body. What still remains to be torn away when the last vestige of clothing has fallen? Where then do this fleshly being, these velvety shapes, these cindery lines take refuge?

They cross a frontier where no gaze can follow them, they escape from hands, they plunge into the sandstorm of oblivion. If a shellfish casing is broken up, reduced to dust, the creature is nowhere to be found. Does not the soul in the same way call to the body, take it into its protection, lend to it its own power of intangibility? If the body is silent, the visage speaks. And it's the visage which we wear, uncovered.

Behold the mystery of a stream which flows freely and clear. But as soon as it's enclosed in a carafe it recognises its nudity, it bares all its secrets. I've come to believe that the body, used for so long to darkness, fears the light and waits for night's large swathes in order to become visible once again. In the gentle and dense darkness the body is like someone who suddenly remembers and turns back, approaches his home, opens the door and announces in a very quiet voice: "Here I am!" Yes, the body comes awake in the night, it is there, it becomes clouded like a visage, it talks, it gives itself up to you.

Close to it you must remain silent, to see how gradually it becomes phosphorescent; it gives out more and more radiance, finally lighting up violently like an unexpected star. A vast and deep sky weaves around the body which, unconstrained, mingles with the other stars and sings a song which intoxicates the universe.

⁂

There is still much to be said about invisibility. This, for example (which I am only noting here). We imagine the invisible and visible connected by a one-sided dependence. That is to say: we don't see the invisible, but the invisible sees us. That must be incorrect. I imagine rather two totally closed worlds ignorant of each other. Those which are visible can see each other but are invisible to the world which we call invisible. Those which are invisible can see each other but can perceive nothing of the other world, the visible, which is in its turn invisible to them. Thus, knowing nothing of one another these two worlds are side by side and even mingle together.

Beneath the same roof, in the same room, a physical family sometimes lives alongside an invisible family. Do they take their meals at the same time, do they go to bed when it's night-time, do they go outside together when the sun shines? I don't believe they use the same furniture and the same utensils. Some weird signs occasionally make people say that these houses are haunted. But you should not trust these signs. The fact that some unusual noises give rise to the suspicion of an invisible presence does not mean that the invisible one lives there. The invisible ones walk around, act, speak and play as we do. They go from one house to another. But their dwelling is superimposed on ours like a halo, like a photographic superimposition. They are to visible beings and objects like their own shadows: light, unstable, intangible.

If some other being with extraordinary sensory powers could see the invisible and the visible at the same time (I've said that being able to see one excludes being able to see the other) an unforgettable sight would reveal itself to his gaze. He would see how in the kitchen, in the dining room, in the bedroom, the visible and the invisible become disentangled and sometimes, without realising it, help each other out. Meals prepared by the invisible ones for their families are sometimes eaten by the visible ones. And vice versa. A weary ghost coming back from a distant errand mistakes a sleeping place and lies down in the bed of a visible one. Or perhaps the head of a family comes home tipsy after celebrating pay day with a few friends and gets into the bed of an invisible one; he then becomes ethereal and his family think they've lost him. Other adventures are kept secret by those experiencing them. They remember nothing, for memory is fashioned in such a way that it only retains those things which relate to its own shape. The rest is lost.

That's why the invisible and the visible forget all about these confused situations. Only a third being controlling both worlds could see all of that and take pleasure in it.

Obviously, it happens that more tragic events occur: that an invisible one falls in love with a visible. Without knowing that their corporeality is so different they each have a hazy, too vague image of the other (for they can't see each other) but they suffer from the feeling of being ignored for the visible one seems distant and unresponsive to the gentle gestures of the invisible one.

It is just a question of very imprecise perceptions. The visible (or the invisible) one has intuited the invisible (or visible) being. Then his search for the other ebbs away and as the two worlds are completely separate they can never be reunited. And then, such sadness and nostalgia! We know a few of these dramas of the visible world: such as a young girl languishing away, the adolescent boy dying of love for a dreamed-of being. But the invisible ones suffer in the same way. And I can easily imagine an old invisible mother, who knows a little witchcraft and who in the course of her wise life has learned things of which the ordinary run of invisibles are unaware, bending over a beautiful adolescent invisible girl who is pining for a real being she has dreamed of, and offering her words of consolation. And perhaps she sometimes succeeds, by making use of very powerful spells, in bringing the beloved young man from the visible world to the invisible world.

How have the invisible ones organised their lives? Do they have working hours as we do? Do they relax after their work by going to funfairs or to the theatre? We are not just in the realm of conjecture here. For I can clearly see the joys of the invisible ones. And aside from love's torments—in love's very joy there is a shade of sadness—they do not suffer other torments. To be precise, they do not know about work. Invisible things have unlimited flexibility and breadth.

Invisible ones, who enjoy a much more developed ability to think than we have, have the possibility of surrounding themselves with a thousand imaginary things. They don't have to construct with their own hands the objects they need, as we do. With their continual mobility and capacity for transformation they become the very things that they imagine. Thus, a simple small invisible girl knows more than the most knowledgeable of our old men. From that follows an easy life, for life can only be comfortable thanks to a depth of knowledge. As for us, what do we know of our world? We have never been able to place ourselves right in the midst of the things which surround us in order to embrace their shapes and to truly know them. Every desire of an invisible one turns it into the desired thing. And do we still know how to desire? Not only have we lost the power of making new objects appear through the strength of our thoughts, but even those things which already exist we despise and ignore. All we do is distance ourselves from the world around us. Our clothes isolate us from the wind and the sun. Our vehicles detach us from the ground. Our ships come between us and the sea.

Imagine one of us suddenly enters the world of the invisible beings where everything is new to him. The invisible ones crowd around him and ask, "Where are you from? Tell us about the world you just left." Then he mentions the flowers, the rain, the wind, the snow. "Describe them for us," the invisible ones say to him. And then he suddenly realises that he knows nothing about all these things. He wants to speak of the wind but he can't. "It's a great breath, a sharp movement of the air." "And the air, what's that? So it's a person like us, like you, who takes his hat and his cane and moves around? Who runs for a tram?" "No, the wind is something else." "So it's a bell which chimes in the night and wakes the stars, making them drop their heavy meteors?" "Oh no, the wind is something else." And as he isn't able to become the wind himself he will be ashamed and confess his ignorance.

"And the mountains, what do you know of them? And the seas? And the forests?" Ah! He'll remember that day when, crossing a meadow, the thistles had stuck to his clothes. He had soon removed them, pulling off small silky balls. But in the following days he found more of them in a fold of his clothes or a greyish flower in a pocket. Perhaps these thistles were no more than messengers from that vast expanse of nature which he would always rush through and which was begging him to stop, to offer it love.

He remembers too the horses' blinkers. He thought himself the master, forcing the brave mares to see no more in front of them than a small stretch of the horizon, but someone even more powerful had put blinkers on him too. And he had been able to see nothing of the things around him. If eyes had blinkers, the other senses were in turn veiled over. A mist had risen between him and the world. An inexplicable haste propelled him along a path the sides of which were separated by high walls. In other words he walked through a tunnel—knowing nothing of the wind, nor of the sun, nor of the stars, nor of snow, nor of plants. Certainly, there were botanists who described the smallest parts of a flower. Astronomers announced eclipses of the moon, geographers spoke of islands resembling large raindrops in the middle of oceans. But all their descriptions were of the outside. In other words, no one knew anything. The man's face will be suffused with sadness. "No, my friend," the invisible ones will cry, "forget about your forgetting (for the memory of forgetting is painful). Think no more of your ignorance. Join in our games." And suddenly the man will lighten up, he will become whatever he chooses, cloud or perfume or music. But then he will stop being visible.

⁂

Push tolerance as far as tolerating the intolerant.

⁂

Truth is a single thing, a lie is multifaceted.

Truth is arid and sober. He who wishes to lie is never satisfied with the lie he prepares. He constructs two, three, ten, he tries them out one after the other. You would say that once his imagination is let loose nothing more can stop him. In short, the liar is seeking after perfection. There is a creative power there.

So what is the first lie that the God of creation uttered and which obliged him thereafter to invent other lies. From what anguish was he suffering, what fault had he to hide so that he became so embroiled, so that he had later to invent the oceans and the earth, and then to people them with fishes, plants, animals, mountains, vines?

The liar's imagination works unceasingly upon those around him and upon himself. Are not all those organs, all those moods which form our being, a tissue of lies? There was once somewhere a tiny dot which wanted to justify its existence, which sought an alibi and became a heart and blood which in their turn invented a brain, a stomach, the liver, the kidneys, the limbs. Dissatisfied with himself, seeking greater perfection, this being invented another being and then another, he surrounded himself with crowds, with towns. So how far away is the truth. The truth is a little seed. The lie is the immense tree which has grown, which blots out the sky, which mocks truth and throws tons of seeds in the eyes of the universe.

Everything I imagine exists. So what exists is greater than what I imagine.

This town, a friend used to tell me, was formerly a place full of fun. No pleasure was forbidden here. And to convince me he told me: One evening I went with some friends to a house where behind great windows disguised as mirrors we witnessed the amorous exploits of a prostitute and a passing punter. I was greatly impressed by this: the man certainly did not suspect that behind that wardrobe strangers were spectators of his transports. But when he had exhausted his vigour and to get dressed and to knot his tie he came up to the mirror everyone, and I especially, was seized with dread: He was looking into mirror as if he had spotted us. We had made efforts to stifle our laughter and our impulse to cry out when, believing himself to be unobserved, the man had climbed onto the woman he desired. And now our presence was going to be revealed. I held my breath. My friends did the same. The man stretched out his arms, smoothed his hair, smiled at himself when we thought he was smiling at us, turned round. We breathed a sigh relief. But we had gone through a strange moment.

I have often thought about that adventure. And I have come to believe that we are all like that man who thinking himself unobserved—save by his accomplice, but accomplices don't see anything—indulged in activities that otherwise he would have kept hidden. There is always someone, a single person or many—there is a crowd of people watching us. Behind that mirror there is someone. In that calm water there are thousands of eyes. In that furniture, in those walls, in those trees, there are beings hiding who can see everything we do. And they must find the faces we pull ridiculous, they must be astonished at our behaviour. It's when we think we're most alone that these invisible beings see and judge us. Here is a man who in day-to-day life is serious, important, moving with his head held high among the humble ranks of his subordinates. In the evening, in his bedroom, he undresses, he removes his wig which lent a slightly youthful look to his lined face, he takes his false teeth out of his mouth, he contemplates his bloated stomach, rumpled like a worn-out piece of material. "No one can see me," he says to himself, and he's glad of it. But no, behind a curtain there are innumerable eyes of those he has ridiculed, humiliated and distressed.

They are all there, holding their breath so as not to reveal their presence. And they can contemplate at their leisure all the degradation, the hideous appearance of this individual who has dominated and ill treated them. Ah! So it's when he thinks he's alone, when he admits to himself his own baseness, that the crowd arrives and listens to his confession. Tomorrow as day breaks this wretched character will resume his proud demeanour, will look scornfully around him, will crush the innocent and the weak, hold out his boots to the servants and give orders in a harsh voice, whilst saying to himself: no one knows what I was thinking of myself last night in front of my mirror. But his game is over: they all pretend to listen to him, to fear him. They seem to be gratifying his needs, to be obeying his orders. But each one knows how greatly this eminent person is lacking in beauty and strength.

Genuine sensitivity: pretending not to notice insensitivity of others.

Do not the shadows follow us like a wild animal
Waiting for a moment's weakness to attack us?
You the shadow who, filled with love and hate, wraps
[yourself around my knees
Dragging me towards the earth where I shall lie and
[never more leave you.

Whilst we are walking with our faces to the sun, our shadows are scratching the earth, seeking the places where they will dig our graves. The places will need to be to their liking of course. So they take years to find them. That is to triumph over death.

We never take enough precautions with the dead. We nail down their coffins, we pile earth and heavy stones onto these and yet, craftier than Houdini, the dead escape and haunt our dwellings.

I had been freed in the world that is vast
So that I could be tiny
I was shut into this tomb that is tiny
So that there I could be vast.

A PARTIAL LIST OF SNUGGLY BOOKS

MAY ARMAND BLANC *The Last Rendezvous*
G. ALBERT AURIER *Elsewhere and Other Stories*
CHARLES BARBARA *My Lunatic Asylum*
S. HENRY BERTHOUD *Misanthropic Tales*
LÉON BLOY *The Tarantulas' Parlor and Other Unkind Tales*
ÉLÉMIR BOURGES *The Twilight of the Gods*
CYRIEL BUYSSE *The Aunts*
JAMES CHAMPAGNE *Harlem Smoke*
FÉLICIEN CHAMPSAUR *The Latin Orgy*
BRENDAN CONNELL *Unofficial History of Pi Wei*
BRENDAN CONNELL *Metrophilias*
RAFAELA CONTRERAS *The Turquoise Ring and Other Stories*
ADOLFO COUVE *When I Think of My Missing Head*
QUENTIN S. CRISP *Aiaigasa*
LUCIE DELARUE-MARDRUS *The Last Siren and Other Stories*
LADY DILKE *The Outcast Spirit and Other Stories*
CATHERINE DOUSTEYSSIER-KHOZE
The Beauty of the Death Cap
ÉDOUARD DUJARDIN *Hauntings*
BERIT ELLINGSEN *Now We Can See the Moon*
ERCKMANN-CHATRIAN *A Malediction*
ALPHONSE ESQUIROS *The Enchanted Castle*
ENRIQUE GÓMEZ CARRILLO *Sentimental Stories*
DELPHI FABRICE *Flowers of Ether*
DELPHI FABRICE *The Red Spider*
BENJAMIN GASTINEAU *The Reign of Satan*
EDMOND AND JULES DE GONCOURT *Manette Salomon*
REMY DE GOURMONT *From a Faraway Land*
REMY DE GOURMONT *Morose Vignettes*
GUIDO GOZZANO *Alcina and Other Stories*
GUSTAVE GUICHES *The Modesty of Sodom*
EDWARD HERON-ALLEN *The Complete Shorter Fiction*
EDWARD HERON-ALLEN *Three Ghost-Written Novels*
RHYS HUGHES *Cloud Farming in Wales*
J.-K. HUYSMANS *The Crowds of Lourdes*
J.-K. HUYSMANS *Knapsacks*
COLIN INSOLE *Valerie and Other Stories*
JUSTIN ISIS *Pleasant Tales II*

VICTOR JOLY *The Unknown Collaborator and Other Legendary Tales*
GUSTAVE KAHN *The Mad King*
MARIE KRYSINSKA *The Path of Amour*
BERNARD LAZARE *The Mirror of Legends*
BERNARD LAZARE *The Torch-Bearers*
MAURICE LEVEL *The Shadow*
JEAN LORRAIN *Errant Vice*
JEAN LORRAIN *Fards and Poisons*
JEAN LORRAIN *Masks in the Tapestry*
JEAN LORRAIN *Monsieur de Bougrelon and Other Stories*
JEAN LORRAIN *Nightmares of an Ether-Drinker*
JEAN LORRAIN *The Soul-Drinker and Other Decadent Fantasies*
GEORGES DE LYS *An Idyll in Sodom*
GEORGES DE LYS *Penthesilea*
ARTHUR MACHEN *N*
ARTHUR MACHEN *Ornaments in Jade*
CAMILLE MAUCLAIR *The Frail Soul and Other Stories*
CATULLE MENDÈS *Bluebirds*
CATULLE MENDÈS *For Reading in the Bath*
CATULLE MENDÈS *Mephistophela*
ÉPHRAÏM MIKHAËL *Halyartes and Other Poems in Prose*
LUIS DE MIRANDA *Who Killed the Poet?*
OCTAVE MIRBEAU *The Death of Balzac*
CHARLES MORICE *Babels, Balloons and Innocent Eyes*
GABRIEL MOUREY *Monada*
DAMIAN MURPHY *Daughters of Apostasy*
KRISTINE ONG MUSLIM *Butterfly Dream*
OSSIT *Ilse*
CHARLES NODIER *Outlaws and Sorrows*
HERSH DOVID NOMBERG *A Cheerful Soul and Other Stories*
PHILOTHÉE O'NEDDY *The Enchanted Ring*
YARROW PAISLEY *Mendicant City*
GEORGES DE PEYREBRUNE *A Decadent Woman*
HÉLÈNE PICARD *Sabbat*
URSULA PFLUG *Down From*
JEREMY REED *When a Girl Loves a Girl*
JEREMY REED *Bad Boys*
ADOLPHE RETTÉ *Misty Thule*
JEAN RICHEPIN *The Bull-Man and the Grasshopper*
DAVID RIX *A Blast of Hunters*
FREDERICK ROLFE (Baron Corvo) *Amico di Sandro*

FREDERICK ROLFE (Baron Corvo) *An Ossuary of the North Lagoon and Other Stories*
JASON ROLFE *An Archive of Human Nonsense*
ARNAUD RYKNER *The Last Train*
MARCEL SCHWOB *The Assassins and Other Stories*
MARCEL SCHWOB *Double Heart*
CHRISTIAN HEINRICH SPIESS *The Dwarf of Westerbourg*
BRIAN STABLEFORD (editor) *Decadence and Symbolism: A Showcase Anthology*
BRIAN STABLEFORD (editor) *The Snuggly Satyricon*
BRIAN STABLEFORD (editor) *The Snuggly Satanicon*
BRIAN STABLEFORD *Spirits of the Vasty Deep*
COUNT ERIC STENBOCK *Love, Sleep & Dreams*
COUNT ERIC STENBOCK *Myrtle, Rue & Cypress*
COUNT ERIC STENBOCK *The Shadow of Death*
COUNT ERIC STENBOCK *Studies of Death*
MONTAGUE SUMMERS *The Bride of Christ and Other Fictions*
MONTAGUE SUMMERS *Six Ghost Stories*
GILBERT-AUGUSTIN THIERRY *The Blonde Tress and The Mask*
GILBERT-AUGUSTIN THIERRY *Reincarnation and Redemption*
DOUGLAS THOMPSON *The Fallen West*
TOADHOUSE *Gone Fishing with Samy Rosenstock*
TOADHOUSE *Living and Dying in a Mind Field*
TOADHOUSE *What Makes the Wave Break?*
LÉO TRÉZENIK *Decadent Prose Pieces*
RUGGERO VASARI *Raun*
ILARIE VORONCA *The Confession of a False Soul*
JANE DE LA VAUDÈRE *The Demi-Sexes and The Androgynes*
JANE DE LA VAUDÈRE *The Double Star and Other Occult Fantasies*
JANE DE LA VAUDÈRE *The Mystery of Kama and Brahma's Courtesans*
JANE DE LA VAUDÈRE *Three Flowers and The King of Siam's Amazon*
JANE DE LA VAUDÈRE *The Witch of Ecbatana and The Virgin of Israel*
AUGUSTE VILLIERS DE L'ISLE-ADAM *Isis*
RENÉE VIVIEN AND HÉLÈNE DE ZUYLEN DE NYEVELT *Faustina and Other Stories*
RENÉE VIVIEN *Lilith's Legacy*
RENÉE VIVIEN *A Woman Appeared to Me*
ILARIE VORONCA *The Confession of a False Soul*
TERESA WILMS MONTT *In the Stillness of Marble*
TERESA WILMS MONTT *Sentimental Doubts*
KAREL VAN DE WOESTIJNE *The Dying Peasant*

Lightning Source UK Ltd.
Milton Keynes UK
UKHW010655221221
396068UK00001B/13